Threatened Species

a novella and five stories

Jeff Vande Zande

WHISTLING SHADE PRESS

PO Box 7084   St. Paul   MN   55107
www.whistlingshade.com

First Edition, First Printing
March 2010

Copyright © 2009 by Jeff Vande Zande
All rights reserved

Some stories in this collection have appeared, in slightly different versions, in the
following publications:

Blue Collar Review
Bravado
Fifth Wednesday Journal
Noun Versus Verb
Parting Gifts
Smokelong Quarterly
Whistling Shade

ISBN 978-0-9800375-7-3

Book and cover design by Joel Van Valin

Printed in the United States of America

For Jennifer, as always.

Threatened Species

One

Through the van's windshield Dad was a silhouette. He walked bent, one hand groping, the other filling with thin shadows that looked like rose stems. "Kindling," I said. I liked the word. He'd said it before getting out. He'd told me to wait. "Just look at the bridge," he'd said.

I'd be with him for two weeks. Mom and John left this morning. Marquette to Chicago to New York to Paris. We'd be moving there in August. John's new job. "Paris," Mom sighed, her eyes far away. She said it a lot.

Dad told her we'd be here, camped on the beach near St. Ignace.

"We're going to heat up pasties in the coals of the campfire," I said.

Mom stood, arms akimbo. "I'm not surprised."

"He doesn't worry so much about the expense of things," he said. He put his fingers in my hair. "So what happens to every other weekend?"

Mom shrugged.

Lit, the Mackinac Bridge looked to be floating in the darkness. Dad was almost gone. If I tried, I could see him crouched by the fire pit. I waited for a flame. When it didn't come, I turned on the CB. Channel 19. "Where the lonely look for the lonely," Dad always said. There were more voices here, near the bridge, than I'd ever heard before. Deep, accented, foul-mouthed and misted over by a static that made them otherworldly. So many voices.

"It's the confluence of every U.P. highway," Dad said when we came down U.S. 2 and the bridge materialized in the southeastern distance. I sucked my milk shake. Dad talked about slow ferries, the straits freezing over, the importance of connection. "Had to have some kind of bridge," he said.

When we pulled into the campsite, he asked me if I liked John. I shook my head. I lied. Dad looked out at the water for a long time.

"Does he treat you okay?"

I nodded.

I couldn't see him anymore. The bridge made everything else darker. No fire yet. No tent.

The driver's door opened, and Dad pulled in behind the wheel. A chill came in with him, and I shivered.

He stared at the bridge. "Let's cross it," he said.

"Okay."

He started the van. The fire pit appeared in the headlights. No fire in it, but the twigs and small branches leaned against each other, tepee style. Kindling. He'd slid birch bark into some of the spaces, left others open. "The space is as important as the wood," he told me four years ago. Mom had listened, shaking her head. "He's too young for fires," she'd said.

"A fire survives on fuel and space," he explained. "Too much of either kills it. It's a balancing game."

The bridge hummed beneath us. Dad told me they vented the middle lanes to keep high winds from tearing it apart.

The van's vents blew cold air. I shivered again. The lights of Mackinaw City glowed dimly ahead of us. The darkness beyond it was much bigger. "Where we gonna camp at?" I asked.

He told me he didn't know.

Two

Dad's hands made small movements on the steering wheel. In my side vision, in the glow of the dashboard, his outline was like a ghost. He hadn't said anything since we crossed the bridge. He didn't even turn on the radio. I hummed a song that was almost always in my head, one Mom and I sometimes sang together.

"You can sleep," he said, "if you want."

I told him I wasn't tired.

"Hungry?"

I shook my head and then told him no.

A few seconds passed. "Are you scared?" he asked, turning toward me for a moment and then back to the road.

I wasn't sure what he meant. "No," I said.

"It's just that your mother doesn't like to drive at night."

I thought about it. It didn't make sense. "She drives at night, now," I said. "She drives to Houghton sometimes after work. John works at the Houghton hospital once a month. They meet at a place called the Library when he gets done. It's a restaurant, though."

"That's fine," Dad said. Then he didn't say anything for a long time.

I closed my eyes. The van was warm and hummed with the passing of the road.

"Grayling," Dad said, waking me.

I opened my eyes, sat up, and looked around. Lights glowed along the edges of the highway. I could see buildings. "What?" I asked.

"Sorry," he said. "It's just a town. Grayling. Named after a fish."

"Grayling?" The lights were becoming more scattered.

He nodded towards the darkness outside his window. "The Au Sable river's out there. It used to be full of these fish. Grayling. Kinda like trout."

"Grayling," I said. Like kindling, I liked to say it.

"Yup," he said. He told me over-fishing had killed them. "They

10

have old fishing journals from the turn of the century. Guys write about catching fifty or sixty grayling a day. Keeping 'em. The fish weren't too bright. They'd jump after anything."

I didn't like that the fish wouldn't come back. I didn't believe it. "There aren't any grayling in the river? How can they know?"

He told me they know. They do tests on the river. He told me they can shock the river and make fish float to the surface. "They haven't found grayling in a long time."

The road was dark again. I thought about the fish. I wanted to see a grayling, and it made me mad that I couldn't. The wolverines bothered me too. And the wolves. I hated stories about animals that were no longer in Michigan. I thought about grayling and stared into the darkness.

"Roscommon," Dad said. "Another town."

I looked but there were no lights. "Where?"

He told me it was a ways off the Interstate. He told me about the south branch of the Au Sable. He told me about some guy named George Mason who had bought up land around the river to protect it. I couldn't really listen to him. My eyes kept closing.

"We'll gas up in West Branch," he said.

"Where are we going to sleep?"

"We really can stay anywhere. You're mine. You're mine for two weeks, right? We can stay anywhere."

"Where are we going to sleep tonight? I'm getting tired." I was getting hungry, too.

He rubbed his hand over his face. "You want to listen to the radio?" He turned it on. He reached over and squeezed my knee. "You listen to the radio," he said. He turned it up. "I'm just going to drive."

I rested my head against my window. I stared into the darkness. I thought of something. "Mom said that you can fly to Paris. She said that there are times in the year when it's not so expensive."

He turned up the radio a little more.

Three

Ed Winters turned towards the on-ramp after gassing up in West Branch. Danny, his son, shifted but did not wake. A pair of headlights glided along the northbound lane towards them, grew brighter, and then disappeared. He checked his rear-view mirror, watching the taillights fade into the distance. When he turned back to the windshield, he was alone in the highway's darkness. The light here was far away, except for the numbered, pale green radiance of the dashboard. The rest was dotted, obscure and cold, glowing dimly out beyond the guardrails. Here, between towns, he would be in the darkness for a long time.

Earlier he'd wanted Danny to sleep. On the road, alone like this, he wanted him awake. He wanted voices, distraction. He'd even take more questions about grayling—anything to keep him from being alone with his thoughts. What were his thoughts? Was he doing this? Was he taking his boy?

Ed glanced over at his son. He was a ghostly outline in the dashboard glow, curled against the passenger door. He could still see him as a young boy. He had given them no terrible twos or threes. He'd been perfect, like a small adult, eager to please. He could stun Ed with a vague smile or unexpected word. Three years old, he had turned from his toys to Ed and Susan on the couch. "I'm very fond of you both," he'd said and then turned back to his play.

Fond. The kid loved words. The kid loved Ed. He said he was going to get a job with the DNR, too. He told Ed that he should sneak him out in a duffel bag, so Ed wouldn't have to do fieldwork alone. He cried not for Susan, but for Ed, at the start of kindergarten.

Ed squeezed the steering wheel. He sniffed and shook off the tears. Those days were over. They would never be back. But in those days he had never questioned what he was doing. Every day unfolded like a map. Sometimes he even felt sorry for people whose marriages fell apart. He knew at one point that he would never be among those people. He knew. He would have Susan and

Danny, and they would be among the lucky who somehow made it. He knew.

What had he known? Why had it seemed so solid? Why did it shatter? The highway was in his headlights, gray just beyond them, and then black ahead. More blackness than anything. It reminded him of coming to bed, rubbing Susan's sleeping back, watching a little Letterman, and then staring up into the endless black of the ceiling.

Sleep never came quickly. He lay in the house and listened. He waited for the perfect silence to be broken. Anything might happen in Danny's room. A nightmare. How many times had he interrupted their lovemaking by pattering down the hall? A cough. Crying. The mumbling of fever. It seldom came when he listened for it, but he knew it was out there. If it didn't come that night, it was certain to come another. It lurked, waiting to bring fear into their lives. Ed could spend a week in a tent in the middle of the Huron Mountains without ever being afraid. At home, the silence coming from his son's room could leave him breathless. He waited, knowing the peace would soon end. It was a temporary state. Anything could trigger it. A flu picked up in day-care might bring midnight vomiting, a high fever, a call to the pediatrician at one in the morning. Then there'd be the endless wait for a sleepy-voiced callback from the doctor. Even in the minor things there was always the sense that they could lose him. He was a tenuous gift. And, they knew if they lost him, they'd lose everything. They'd invested too much love.

In the darkness just after television, Ed had waited for something. It was out there. It would come. He guessed that they'd always work through it, pray if they had to. He guessed that everything would be okay in the end. He never guessed the divorce. She'd delivered the papers like a sucker punch. "Are you really that surprised?" she'd asked.

Like that it was gone. All of it. He'd known something that had made him feel like everything made some kind of sense. At the end of every day, even the worst days, he was somebody's father. A boy looked to him with hope. A boy waited for him. Then, in a matter of time, the boy lived with his mother in a home that Ed once owned. Ed lived by himself, thousands of miles away, in an apart-ment across town. Everything ended and wouldn't come back—no matter what he tried.

Flint. The roadside glowed with it. Then Fenton. Brighton. There was less darkness, more cars. Ed pushed on vaguely. Look-ing for a motel. Not looking for a motel. Wanting to put miles behind them, and then not caring.

Four

I lifted my head from the window. I rubbed a finger into one eye and a thumb into the other. My shirt was sticking to me, and my face felt damp. Sun came in through the windshield. Blinking, I looked under the light. Other cars were parked in spaces around us. Dad wasn't in his seat.

His voice came from behind me. "Are you up?"

I nodded and then said, "Yes."

He told me he didn't want to wake me because I was sleeping so soundly.

I looked around. A parking lot. Beyond it, grass. Trees. Like a park or something. A woman trotted her dog in the grass until it stopped and squatted. "Where are we?" I asked.

"Just a rest stop. After you fell asleep, I drove for awhile." He asked me if I remembered stopping in West Branch.

"No."

"You woke up for a few seconds. You talked." He told me he had gassed up in West Branch.

I turned around in my seat. He was sitting in the back of the van on an old army cot. He always took the cot camping. "Keeps you off the ground," he always said. His hair looked like all the times I remembered it from mornings when he and mom were together. Sticking up. It made me feel good.

He patted it with his hands. "What?"

I laughed. "I'm hungry," I said.

"You should be hungry, kiddo. We didn't really have dinner last night." He patted the cot, and I came back and sat next to him. He put his arm around me. "What do you want to eat? Pancakes?"

"Waffles," I said.

"Waffles it is." He kept his arm around me.

Heads passed by through the windshield. "Why didn't we camp last night?" I asked.

He took his arm off me and scratched his hair. I could smell his smell now. It wasn't bad. It was just him.

"Too dark and too late by the time we got here," he said.

"Why didn't we camp where we were? By the bridge."

"I don't really know, now," he said. He said something I didn't understand about things looking different in the light. He hugged me for what seemed like longer than ever before. He kissed my head. "Let's get this day started," he said. "Let's get waffles."

He took me up to the bathrooms. We splashed water into our faces, and he wet and combed down his hair. In the mirror I could see him looking at me.

"You didn't mind the drive, did you?"

I shook my head.

He told me he loved taking rides at night with his father. "He had that wrecker," he sighed. "He'd get calls at night, and if I was up he'd take me with him." He said he thought I might like a little ride. "It was fun, right?"

I nodded.

He started the van. I wondered if Mom and John were already in Paris. I asked Dad.

He pulled it into reverse. "Don't know," he said.

The land around the highway was very flat. I could see tiny houses in the distance.

"We'll stop in a bit," he said. "I'm just going to get some miles behind us."

My stomach growled. I looked out the window for a while, but everything looked the same. "Have you ever been to Paris?" I asked.

He shook his head. "My dad—Grandpa—was in Paris during World War II," he said. "But I don't want to talk about Paris," he said. He turned on the radio. "Just think about what you want to do today."

I looked out the window. Sometimes I didn't know what I'd done to make him angry.

We passed a sign that said we were leaving Ohio. Then there was another sign. *Welcome to Michigan. Great Lakes. Great Times.* I looked at Dad, but he stared at the road.

Five

I'd eaten one and a half waffles before I said anything. Dad's spoon hadn't moved from where it sat in his oatmeal. He ran his finger around the rim of his coffee cup. He stared out the window towards the parking lot. I didn't want him to be quiet anymore.

I swallowed. "Jimmy said that I'll get beat up a lot—that French kids don't like American kids. His cousin lives in Quebec, and gets beat up nearly every week."

He looked at me and moved his spoon around in his oatmeal. "Quebec is Canada," he said.

"Jimmy said it's probably the same in France." I wanted Jimmy to be wrong.

"I don't know," Dad said. He blinked his eyes a few times. Every man at the counter was smoking, and the smoke moved sluggishly in the air.

I looked at him, hoping he'd say more.

He took a bite of his oatmeal. He swallowed. "They've got American schools in Paris. You'll be going to school with other American kids. There's lots of Americans living in Paris, and they send their kids to American schools. You'd have to speak French to go to a French school." He put an elbow on the table and rubbed his hand over his chin. "You don't speak French, do you?" he asked. One of his eyebrows went up.

I smiled. I shook my head.

He told me I'd be fine. I felt better. Nobody had told me about the American schools. We ate. Cars pulled into and left the parking lot. Beyond the parking lot, the cars on the interstate were constant. The waitress came by and filled Dad's coffee.

Dad pointed his spoon at me. He asked if anything else about moving to Paris bothered me.

I told him I'd miss my friends. "I'll miss Jimmy."

He nodded. He told me that Jimmy was going to miss me, too. "That's why he said it," he said. "About getting beat up. He's mad that you're leaving. He doesn't have anyone to really be mad at so he's mad at you. He doesn't want you to go."

It didn't make sense, but I nodded.

He put his elbows on the table and touched his fingertips to his lower lip. "Do you want to go?" he asked.

"Not always," I answered. Whenever I talked with Mom, I wanted to go. She could make it seem like a chance anyone would be lucky to get. Then, when I was alone, or in bed at night, I could really get myself feeling that it was the last thing I wanted to do. I told my dad that.

He nodded. "It's hard to think about things in the dark."

I skated my last bite of waffle through the syrup.

"And," Dad said, "your mother has a way of making something she wants sound pretty damn good."

I looked at him.

"And, it probably will be good," he said. "Maybe it'll be the best thing that ever happened to you."

I wasn't really sure what he meant. I chewed my waffle.

Dad reached over and took a sausage from my plate. He bit a piece from it and chewed for a moment. "But what if," he started. "What if you didn't have to go? Would that be easier?"

"What?"

He took a sip of his coffee. "I mean, if John decided not to take the job. Would you be happier to stay right here in Michigan?"

I thought about it. I nodded.

He smiled.

The waitress came by and set the check on the table. "There you go, darling."

"Darling?" Dad said, smiling. "Do you think you should be calling me darling in this day and age?"

The waitress looked at him. "I call everyone darling."

"Well now I'm really offended," Dad said. "You made me think *I* was your darling."

The waitress smiled, shook her head, walking away. Dad watched her. He picked up his cup and tipped the last of his coffee into his mouth. He swallowed. He rapped the cup down on the table. "What would you think of going fishing today? I see you brought your fishing pole."

"I brought my rod," I corrected. John made a big deal about calling it a rod.

Dad nodded. "Good," he said. He took out his wallet and set some bills down on the check. "We'll take you and your rod up to the Rifle River."

I followed him out to the van. "Maybe we'll catch a grayling," I said.

He looked at me. "What? I told you there aren't any grayling left in Michigan."

"We'll see," I said. That was something John always said.

Dad sniffed a little laugh through his nose. He whistled for a while on the interstate. Then, after a time, he stopped.

Six

I pulled the line through the guides. I checked to make sure I didn't miss any. Then I checked the length of my leader and tippet. They were good. I took a fly from my vest and started to tie it on. Dad had been really quiet ever since I took the rod out of the case and told him, when he asked, that John was teaching me how to fly fish.

"Rifle's a good trout stream," he finally said. "It's not good in July, but early in the season like this, or later, it can be as good as any of them."

I nodded.

"You should be able to wade it, too. There are some deep holes, but there's shallow water all around. You can work the holes from the shallow water."

I pulled my waders on.

In the current, I could feel him watching me. My casting was bad at first, but got better. I wanted it to be good.

He stopped watching and worked his spinners through the holes. I did what I could to work the surface.

"Now this one's a better one," Dad shouted. He reeled in the fish. He walked it over to me. Then he told me to follow him onto shore, where he bent down and rapped the squirming fish's head against a rock. It stopped moving. "Do you know how to tell one trout from another?"

I shook my head.

"Hmm. John must not have had time to teach you that yet." He opened his hand and the fish lay in his palm. "This is a brookie," he said. He told me there were signs. Squared tail. Wormy marks on its back. Reddish spots with blue halos. "Forget all that. You see these lower fins? Pinkish with a bright white stripe. Brookie. No other trout looks like this." He dropped the fish in his creel. "I love those white stripes. You can see 'em even before you get the fish out of the water. Beautiful."

"What about the others?"

"Browns and rainbow? Browns have spots all over. No wormy

marks. They always look kinda yellowish to me on the bottom. Definitely no white stripe." He told me rainbow have an obvious stripe running down the middle of each side of them. "Plus they've got white mouths," he said.

"And no white stripe on the lower fins, right?" I said.

"Exactly."

We went back to fishing. I worked over in my head what he had told me. I wanted to have it memorized.

An hour passed with no fish.

"If you wanted to camp around here," Dad started, "there are some good bass and perch lakes nearby. We could rent a little boat, pack a lunch. I've got an extra pole if you want to take an afternoon and drown some worms."

Dad's legs were gone beneath the surface. I thought for a moment. I shook my head.

"Oh no," he laughed. "He's already a trout snob."

It wasn't much later that something took my fly under. I didn't do what John said I should do, but I was lucky and the fish hooked itself. My heart pounded something tingly through me. I remembered to strip the line in and not use the reel. I remembered to lighten my tension when the fish fought too hard. I landed it. White stripes on the lower fins. A nice nine-inch brookie.

Dad told me how well I did. "Let me try your rod," he said. "I've been watching you. I think I can do it."

He went out to the middle and started to cast. For a while, the line did nothing, but then he figured out enough to get it moving. When he found a rhythm, the line snapped the water behind him and in front of him. He tried, but could not get rid of the snap.

I laughed.

He waded the rod back to me. "Okay, what's so funny?" he asked, smiling.

"You're like a lion tamer out there. That's what John would say," I said.

He looked at me, and his face changed. "Well," he said, "I wouldn't laugh too much. Let's not forget who taught you how to fish to begin with. You weren't too good for perch back then."

He was angry with me again. He fished fast downstream away

from me. He went around a bend. When I came around the same bend, he was nowhere in the river, already gone around another bend. I was afraid of the deeper holes without him in the water near me. I stopped fishing, moving faster to try to catch up with him. I had to take wide, funny steps, and the water tangled between my legs. My eyes watered. After nearly falling in, I stopped. I tried to calm myself.

In my creel, my brookie was already losing its color and detail. It looked foggy. Its white stripes were harder to see.

Seven

Ed Winters needed crackers. He needed butter. He was happy to have these simple needs. The small convenience store had both. Near the entrance, Danny ran his fingers over the glass top of a display case filled with hand-tied flies. Ed had seen them on the way in. Brown Drake and Hex patterns. Even though he didn't fly fish, he knew the June hatches. Old friends of his from his DNR days were avid fly fishermen.

Today was a good day. He'd landed five nice brookies between eight and ten inches. Danny had landed one also. They'd landed a meal's worth. Smiling, Ed grabbed a bag of potatoes. He'd slice them thin and fry them up. Makeshift french fries.

French. France. Paris. Susan, his ex, and John in Paris. John nailing Susan near an open window of their hotel room with the street sounds of Paris coming into the room. Something as small as french fries brought his mind here.

He'd grown used to the idea of Susan being with another man. He could live with it. Another thought loomed larger in his mind, a thought he could barely live with. Danny was leaving in less than two months. He would live in another country. The boy was only ten feet from him now, but Ed could already feel what it would be like to live with that distance. John would become Danny's dad. Ed would become his biological father. "What, my real dad?" he imagined Danny saying. "I see him every three or four years. He's in the States." The idea stopped his breath. He worked hard to swallow.

"Dad?"

Ed looked down at his son. "What?"

"Can I get a pop?"

Ed pushed a palm into his teary eyes. "Of course, bud. Get whatever you want."

Danny jogged off towards the coolers, his gait loose and untrained. He was still a boy, excited for the moment over a pop.

Ed snapped a quick nod to himself. No more dwelling on what

lies ahead, he decided. Danny was here. They had fish, and they would cook them. They'd sit up late around the fire. They'd talk and have conversations that Danny would remember.

A new thought came to Ed. It made him oddly happy, and he moved to the next aisle. Tartar sauce. He almost always forgot it, but this time he hadn't. He'd finally got one over on his memory.

Not finding it right away, he looked through the dressings. Ranch, Thousand Island, Italian, Vinaigrette, French.

French.

He skipped the tartar sauce and stopped by the cooler. Along with the crackers, butter, and potatoes, he set a twelve pack of beer next to the cash register.

Eight

Dad stirred the coals and pushed the logs into different positions. Flames flickered up, and our small circle of warm light grew a little brighter. Dad opened another beer from his box. We stared into the fire. When I looked up from it, everything else was black with darkness, the sky blue-black. I wished Dad would say something. Our tent wasn't far away, but I couldn't see it. I reached down next to my chair and touched my flashlight.

"The fish were good, weren't they?" Dad asked. His voice was different, a little wobbly. Happy.

I could only see a dim shape of him in the firelight. "Yeah," I said.

He moved his stick through the coals. I watched, but he didn't put another log on the fire.

"It will be cold tonight," he said. "Got a good sleeping bag? You don't still sleep in that old one of mine, do you?"

"No," I said. I told him we threw it away. "I think the new one I have is pretty good."

He didn't say anything.

We watched the fire again for what seemed like a long time. He stirred it, but no more flames came up from the charred logs. Fire flashed briefly from the coals but never lasted. A question came into my head, and I couldn't get rid of it.

"Why did you leave?" I asked.

Dad's stick stopped moving. "What, today on the river? You mean just for that little bit? I just thought we'd have a better chance at some fish if we split up. The Rifle's tight for two guys to fish like that. I mean, we're big guys. Big guys like us need the river to ourselves."

I told him I didn't mean today.

He opened another beer. Shadows flitted over his head against the paler darkness of the sky. Bats, I guessed.

"I meant after. After you and Mom got divorced, you left." I knew he went to California. I knew he fought fires. I knew that after the fires were out he taught again. But, I didn't know why he'd left in the first place.

I heard him drink.

"Look," he started. "I don't really remember why I left now. But it wasn't because I didn't love you anymore or anything like that." He said getting away from something sometimes seems like the only way to work through it.

I didn't ask any more. I watched the coals and listened to his swallowing.

He flipped his empty beer cans into the fire pit. The lettering melted away and, after a second, the little bit of remaining beer began to sizzle.

"So," he said, "what did your mom say about it? My leaving."

I told him she didn't say anything.

He told me it was a big mistake. "I gave up everything."

I wasn't sure what he meant.

"I want you to know, though, that I came back for you. There wasn't a day out there, even when the fires were at their worst, that I didn't think about you." He set the top of his head into his hands and looked at the ground. "I don't know. I guess I thought if I got away from … I just thought that the love … that the loss wouldn't hurt so much with some distance. And I had nothing when I got back. I had no say in anything. She didn't even have to—"

"Have to what?" I asked.

"Nothing."

The coals crackled faintly.

"Well," he said, "why don't you get in now? We'll do something good tomorrow. Something fun."

"What?"

"I don't know, but it will be fun. It has to be. But now just get into the tent." He told me he'd be in soon.

I followed my flashlight.

"Danny?"

I turned, and he shielded his eyes. I turned the light off.

He told me to give him a kiss good-night. I worked slowly through the darkness to get to him, keeping my eyes on the coals. I smelled the beer when I kissed his stubbly cheek. He told me he loved me.

"I love you too, Dad." He hugged me with his head against my chest for a long time. He told me again that he loved me.

The insides of the sleeping bag warmed around me. My legs were tired from walking in the river. I was tired. I closed my eyes and saw the brook trout I caught that day. My first fish on a fly. I wondered what John would say.

I jumped awake when Dad cracked another beer.

Nine

Something woke me, startled me, but I wasn't sure what, and I wasn't sure of where I was. Sound shished around me when I moved. Then I remembered. Sleeping bag. The tent. Dad. Camping somewhere near the Rifle River.

I knew he wasn't inside before I even started to feel around for him. His sleeping bag was cold and flat.

Coyotes howled from somewhere not too far away. I bolted right up. Their high-pitched calling collided and did crazy things in my ears, like when little kids scream as loud as they can together. I guessed there were a hundred of them. I'd heard them once when camping with Dad and Mom in the past, but not so close. My heart wanted out of my ribs.

After their noise faded, I listened for a long time. I didn't hear anything. Then I heard Dad.

"Stupid," he hissed. "Stupid sonuvabitch."

I unzipped the tent. Blackness. Where the fire had been there was only the faintest glow. I turned my flashlight on, and Dad appeared. Face in hands. Elbows on knees.

"Turn it off," he said after a few seconds.

I did.

The coyotes howled again. Faded.

"They wake you up?"

"There's a lot of them, and they're close," I said.

He told me that they howl to warn other coyotes off their territory. "And, their packs aren't very big. Usually just little families of four or five. A few can sound like fifty once they start howling."

"Do they ever attack people?"

He snorted a laugh. "Hell no. They're skittish as hell." He stood up. I heard his zipper, and then I heard him peeing. "They're interesting, though. Sometimes a badger and a coyote will work together to get prey. A coyote will sniff out a hole, and the badger will burrow in. Usually after a squirrel. If the squirrel pops up out of another hole, the coyote nails him. Then they share. The badger and the coyote share."

He finished peeing and zipped up. "I mean, how do they work that out? A coyote and a badger. Do they sit down and talk about it? Do they have a little flip pad and use Xs and Os and lines to plot out their plan of attack?" He laughed.

I liked the idea of the badger and the coyote working together. I felt better and wasn't afraid anymore.

Dad moved towards the tent. I heard him stumble. He steadied himself. "How the hell is it that a goddamn coyote and badger can make things work?" he said.

He didn't move well inside the tent. Taking off his clothes, he fell on me twice. He wrestled and kicked his way into his sleeping bag. He called it a goddamned thing.

A few minutes passed. He didn't move around anymore. I closed my eyes. The coyotes howled again, but I didn't care. It was fun listening to them, imagining the small family in some meadow nearby. They would hunt together.

"Another thing, too" Dad said into the darkness. "Coyotes mate for life. Like wolves. It's not always like that."

Ten

I opened my eyes to the darkness. I heard and felt Dad snoring next to me. The tent smelled like beer. Gross beer. I pulled my cold head into the sleeping bag.

Closing my eyes tightly, I tried to think of anything other than sleep. Sleep would happen if I didn't lie and think about it. I thought about Mom and John and where they might be in Paris. They were finding us an apartment, but it was hard to imagine where they were because I couldn't imagine Paris. The Eiffel Tower came into my mind, but nothing else. Sleep didn't come either.

The cold. Dad's snoring. They wouldn't let me sleep. And there was something else. It was a feeling that I was so alone, here in the cold dark. I could tell by his snoring that even if I could wake him, Dad would be groggy. He'd mumble and keep falling back to sleep. I'd feel even more alone.

The thought came as a feeling at first, something I really couldn't name but, like the Mackinac Bridge, it materialized into something solid, something real. I was moving. Not to another town. Not to another state. To another country that I couldn't even imagine when I closed my eyes. People wore berets and they hated Americans. This is what I knew. Lying in the cold darkness of the tent, I imagined Paris as the coldest, saddest place any kid from America could move to.

Mom would come back in a week and a half. We were going to have a big sale. "We're going to have to sell the non-essential stuff," John told us. "We're going to have to be mercenary about it." I didn't know what that meant, but it turned out to mean that we'd be selling my bike, most of my toys, my desk, and my bed. "We'll get new things," Mom said. "This stuff is old anymore. How exciting to get all new things."

Pulled inside the dark sleeping bag, I wanted old things. I wanted the old bottle collection that John said was just too heavy. Jimmy and I had spent two summers digging them out of the ground near the edge of the dump. I wanted to wake up in my bed and find Jimmy standing at the foot of it. I wanted his smile and his glasses and him telling me that we'd follow the pipeline trail on our bikes farther than we ever had before. I wanted to know that he would always be my friend. I didn't want to write "long, wonderful" letters like Mom said.

And I didn't want what I could feel coming. I didn't want to cry. It would take me like a storm if I let it.

I shook him and said, "Dad." I pushed on his back with both hands and tried to roll him around. When he stopped snoring for a moment, I thought he'd wake. Then he rolled onto his back, and the snoring came again. Louder. More like an animal snarling a warning than a snore. I wanted him to wake and say things that would make me feel better, but he was gone.

I pressed my face into my pillow and let it come.

Eleven

The trees along US 10 west of Midland reminded Ed Winters of the Upper Peninsula, and for a moment he was overcome by the feeling of coming home. He couldn't get his mind around this feeling. He hadn't considered any place home in over a year. Driving to his sister's house in Ludington felt something like a reunion, but not a homecoming. He couldn't really figure out why this morning, in the grogginess of a hangover, he had announced that he and Danny should go see Aunt Cindy. It put them in the van. It gave them something to do. Ed felt more than anything that he needed to keep doing things.

"Clare," he said.

Danny looked out the window at the northeastern outskirts of the small town.

Ed didn't know anything about the town and didn't say anything else. It soon faded behind them. Highway signs were already advertising the miles left to other towns: Evart and Reed City. Danny went back to the comic book they'd picked up in Standish.

Ed stole glances at his son. The boy's eyes had already improved since the red puffiness of the morning. Tired. That's what Ed guessed. Between one night of sleeping kink-necked against the van door and another night of howling coyotes, his son had to be exhausted. Tonight the boy would sleep in a bed, and the idea made him feel like a better father.

"You could sleep," he said. "We've got a ways to go before Ludington."

Danny shrugged but didn't say anything.

Quiet. Maybe angry or confused. Ed wasn't sure. It wasn't what he wanted. As the road kept coming ahead of them, a sentence kept playing through his mind: When next we meet, son, we will be strangers. He wasn't sure where he'd heard it before. It didn't seem like a sentence that he would put together. It haunted him through the silence.

"Want the radio on?" he asked.

Danny shook his head.

"Don't you feel sick when you read in the car? I can't do it."

"It doesn't bother me," Danny said, not looking up.

Ed nodded. "Well, get some sleep if you want. If you're awake in Reed City and you're hungry, we can stop for lunch."

They passed through Evart, but Ed did not say the name of the town. Speaking even one word seemed too exhausting. Over the last twenty miles a heaviness had settled over him. He had the strength to make the small movements on the wheel that the road required. He had little else. When next we meet, son, we will be strangers.

Danny closed his comic book. "There aren't any grayling?" he asked after a moment. "Not even in the U.P.?"

"Not in Michigan," he managed. "In Alaska there are still grayling." He told him about his old friend who worked in Alaska as a deck boss on a king crab trawler. "I still talk to him sometimes."

Danny was quiet. "That's too far," he finally said.

Ed smiled. The way his son's mind worked sometimes surprised him, even pleased him. "Why this sudden urge to see a grayling?"

"I don't know. Have you ever seen one?"

"Pictures," Ed said. He told his son he didn't remember everything, but he remembered a huge dorsal fin. "It almost looked like a small sailfish." He felt better while talking.

"What about a wolverine? Have you ever seen a wolverine?"

Pictures of different animals blurred in Ed's mind. "Not to describe one, really. I forget, I guess."

Danny didn't say anything. Ed glanced over. The boy was staring out the window.

"I hate that things can just go away like that," Danny said. "Maybe it's stupid, but it makes me mad."

Ed gripped the wheel. He told his son it wasn't stupid.

Twelve

It came into sight slowly. Something green ahead on the side of the road. A sign. White lettering. Then it read clearly. Baldwin was only five miles away.

"Baldwin," Dad said. "We're getting close."

Not much later we crossed the Baldwin River. I tried to see it but couldn't.

Dad told me that downstream the Baldwin had a confluence with the Pere Marquette. "Pere Marquette's a good trout stream," he said.

I asked if the Pere Marquette once had grayling.

"Dunno."

I could see little lakes beyond the shoulder on my dad's side of the road. The blue flashed through the trees. Then the lakes stopped and it was just trees.

"You know that Uncle Kenny and Aunt Cindy don't have kids, right?"

I looked at him glancing over towards me. I nodded.

He reached over and shook my knee. "Try not to bring it up, okay?"

"Bring what up?"

"Nothing. Just don't... don't ask them or anything why they don't have kids."

I told him I wasn't going to.

"I know you weren't," he said. "I didn't think ... it's just that they tried really hard to have kids, but they couldn't. There's no reason to bring it up. I didn't think you would, but I just wanted you to know that you shouldn't is all."

We drove for a few more miles. I asked him why they couldn't have kids.

He exhaled. "I can't really explain it. It's just the way things turn out sometimes. Sometimes people who didn't do anything at all have bad things happen. They can't have kids. That's just the way it happens to be."

I thought about what he said, and I thought about how Jimmy's mom had died from cancer. She was as young as Mom. She hadn't done anything. She didn't even smoke. It didn't seem fair that bad things could happen for no reason. It just seemed to make everything a lot harder for a lot of people.

"Why did you and Mom get divorced?" I asked. The question had always been in my head, but it suddenly seemed like the time to ask it.

"What?"

I didn't repeat the question, and he didn't say anything right away. I could feel him looking at me from time to time.

"What did your mother say about it?"

I told him I never really asked her. We drove for at least another mile.

"It's like anything else," he started. "It's hard to put a finger on why something happens. But it wasn't you. It wasn't your fault at all."

I nodded.

He told me he worked the same question around in his head sometimes. "Sometimes," he said, "to get a simple grip on it, I put things together this way. Your mother fell out of love with me. It happens sometimes. Like anything else."

I listened, but he didn't say more, so I thought about what he had said. Mom didn't love Dad anymore. I didn't know how that happened. It seemed like if it was important, if you had a family, then you stayed in love. You didn't let yourself fall out. Didn't it make it easier on everyone if you just kept loving the person you married? Why fall out of love with Dad to fall into love with John? Why didn't she think about me? Why be so selfish? Coyotes and wolves could mate for life. Why couldn't Mom?

"No, no. Shit!"

I jerked against my seat belt. The van slowed quickly, and Dad turned into a gas station.

He undid his seat belt. "I'll be right out."

When he came back a minute later, he slammed his door. He got back on the road we'd been on, but he went in the other direction.

I asked him what was the matter.

He turned on the radio. "We missed a turn about thirty miles back," he said over the music that was suddenly in the van with us. "You'd think they would have some bigger goddamn signs."

Thirteen

Ludington grew slowly in the distance, and the blue of Lake Michigan stretched out beyond it. Lined with shops and restaurants, the main street dipped and rose. People moved in small groups on the sidewalks, and small children ran ahead pointing. Smiling.

"Pretty little town," Dad said.

The lake kept coming at us, but we turned a few blocks before we reached the beach.

"Stay in the car when we get there," he said. "She's not expecting us, and I just want to talk to her."

The streets were nice and neat, lined as they were with well-manicured lawns and eclectically decorated houses. It reminded me of Marquette. I could sense the lake, even when I couldn't see it.

Dad pulled into a driveway. Up near the bushes of the smaller home, a figure stood. Wearing a large brimmed sun hat, a woman wiped the back of her garden-gloved hand across her forehead. Aunt Cindy. She looked towards the car.

"I'll be just a minute," Dad said. He shifted into park and cut the engine.

Aunt Cindy took off her hat and studied Dad for a moment. "Eddy?" she said, smiling, but I didn't hear anything she said after. He nodded. They both took a few steps forward and hugged. When they stepped back from each other, Dad talked and Aunt Cindy nodded. Dad pointed off in the distance, away from the lake, towards the direction from which we'd come. Then he pointed at the car. He held his hand in the air, and I could tell that he was indicating my height to her. She shook her head and smiled. Her mouth moved.

Dad turned towards the car and motioned me out.

"Danny," Aunt Cindy shouted. "Look at you!"

I hadn't seen her in some time. I stood by the car, looking at the ground.

"Come give your aunt a hug," Dad said.

She wrapped her arms around me and kissed my cheek. Holding my shoulders, she pushed me back slightly and looked at my face. She was pretty and had her blonde hair pulled back into a ponytail. "He's really starting to look like Dad in the face, isn't he?" she said.

Dad looked at me for a moment. "Yeah, I guess he is a bit."

"More than just a bit." She looked my face over again. "Your dad says that you guys are going to stay here for a while."

I nodded.

Dad asked about Uncle Kenny.

"He's at work. He'll go to the gym after work, but he'll be here by six."

"Still hitting the weights, eh?"

"Religiously."

Dad took our things out of the van. The house was small, but they had a guest room for him and a pullout sofa in the living room for me.

We sat out on the back deck with lemonades.

"Jesus Christ," Dad said, looking at me, "he does look like Dad. I never really saw it."

Aunt Cindy smiled and combed her fingers through my hair. "You would have been grandpa's little guy." She looked over at Dad. "He would have loved being a grandpa, don't you think?"

Dad nodded slowly. "He'd a been a damn good one, too."

We were all quiet for a moment, me only because they were.

Aunt Cindy finished the last swallow of her lemonade, and the ice cubes hit her lips. She set the glass down. "What do you want to do first, Danny? We can do whatever you'd like."

"Don't you have to get back to your gardening?" I asked. I wasn't sure why the question had popped out of my mouth.

She shook her head, smiling. "No, it can wait. Why don't we go inside and play a game. Do you like board games?"

I nodded.

"You want to play, Eddy?"

Dad stood up. "No," he said. "I'm going to take a walk down by the lake."

He looked angry again, and didn't look anyone in the eye. He started across the back lawn, and I watched him disappear around the corner of the house. I watched the corner for a moment after he was gone.

"Don't worry about him," Aunt Cindy said. "He's always been moody—even when we were kids. He'll be back in no time."

Aunt Cindy talked like Mom. I felt better.

"What about Monopoly? Do you like Monopoly?"

I told her it was a long game to play.

"Good," she said. "You guys can't leave then until we finish the game. It could take weeks."

Nodding and smiling, I followed her into the house.

Fourteen

It took Ed Winters some time to remember how to walk on a beach. His feet sank, and for a while it was more of a stumbling gait than a walk. He had to stop thinking and concentrate on his feet. He moved closer to the water where the sand was wet, smooth and firm. He walked, moving up and then back with the rhythm of the waves. The small waves hushed against the shore. The sky was overcast, but it wasn't going to rain. At least a mile out, a car ferry made a small shadow on the surface. Ed walked, as though he could keep a step ahead of the heavy feelings, like some stranger walking close behind him. He looked for beach glass, but found none.

When he heard voices, he looked up. A family, in clothes rather than bathing suits, had set up a picnic on the beach. The mother pulled sandwiches out of a basket. The father had his son and daughter, maybe six and eight years old, closer to the water. He pointed out towards the ferry.

Ed turned around and started back down the wet strip of sand. The waves had already erased his footprints, and he smirked to himself. It occurred to him that his whole life was a path of erased footprints.

Who did he have? An ex-wife. A son. Both would be gone in less than two months. His father and mother were already gone. His father died when Ed was sixteen. Driving out at night in a blizzard, he'd gone off the road in the wrecker. No seat belt, he'd put himself through the windshield. That evening, he'd asked Ed to go with him but, already a licensed driver himself, Ed felt he'd outgrown such excursions. Ed's mother had died from a stroke nearly eight years ago. Danny never really knew either of them.

Who else? A sister he rarely saw. Lou Ferrigno for a brother-in-law.

A good distance from the family on the beach, Ed sat in the sand. He rubbed his hands over his face and then scratched his fingers into his scalp. His beard was beyond stubble. His hair felt as though someone had rubbed vegetable oil into it. He'd shower once he got back to Cindy's.

The dark feelings settled over him. What did he have? A double-wide on the swampy end of Big Shag Lake. A shitty job teaching biology at Gwinn High, a job he took only to be closer to Danny.

An osprey that been flying in wide circles over the shallow water finally stooped. It hit the surface, flapped its wings for a few seconds as though keeping balance, and then rose into the air again. It held a fish. The fish moved only slightly, and Ed guessed that it'd been dying on the surface.

The lake stretched out in front of him until it disappeared into the overcast horizon. Nothingness. A cold body of water. Something to drown in.

He stood up, and the words came into his mind: I have nothing. I have nothing. I have nothing. He had no friends in Gwinn. His old friends in Marquette were too far away, and when he did see them they were polite, but cautious. They didn't seem to know how to treat him anymore. Sheila was in California. She wouldn't want anything to do with him. Would she?

Walking again, his foot kicked up a flat stone. He picked it up and wristed it at the surface. He anticipated the skips, but the rock hit the water once and disappeared. Ed tried to take a deep breath, but something seemed to constrict his chest. He aimed himself away from the beach back toward Cindy's.

Walking through the front door, he found the three of them flopped around on the living room floor. Kenny lay on his side resting his head against his hand. Below his ear, his bicep looked like skin wrapped around a cantaloupe. Danny stood by a large flip pad. There were stick figures on it. One figure lay on the ground. With her arms hugged around her knees, Cindy watched Danny intently. They looked like a family.

"Hey, Ed," Kenny said.

"Dad, we're playing Pictionary. Want to play?"

Ed shook his head.

"Come on," Cindy pleaded. "It's a lot better with teams."

He told them he was going to take a shower.

"I haven't showered yet," Kenny offered. "They don't seem to mind."

Cindy held her nose and wafted her hand over her husband. Danny laughed.

"Maybe later. I just want to take a shower, if that's all right. Can I do that?"

They looked at him. Danny's eyes looked hurt.

"Go ahead," Kenny said. "Just leave fifty cents on the kitchen table to pay for the water."

Nobody laughed.

"Maybe I'll play later," Ed said. He walked towards the stairs.

"He's fine," he heard Cindy say. "He'll play later. You'll see. Just keep drawing."

Ed stood on the stairs for a few minutes listening to them.

Fifteen

Darkness pressed at the windows. Drawn by the fluorescent light of the kitchen, June bugs and mosquitoes bounced against the screen. A large moth, like a lost ghost, drifted in from the blackness and then disappeared again. Ed looked towards the living room where he imagined Danny was comfortably asleep.

He put his finger against a June bug on the screen. Its tiny claws picked at his skin. "It's a beetle," he said.

"Yeah?" Kenny asked.

Ed nodded. "They live under ground for about two years after they hatch out of eggs. Maybe you've seen them. They're little white grubs—sometimes come up in a shovelful of dirt in the garden."

Cindy shuddered. "Oh, I don't like them. They're so ugly."

"Good for fishing, though," Kenny said.

Ed nodded. "It's weird. There's this slender black wasp—I forget the name—and it burrows down and finds a June bug grub. It will lay an egg on the grub's back, and then when the wasp larva hatches it will suck the grub's body fluid until it's eaten all of it."

"Ooh, Eddy, gross," Cindy exclaimed, shrugging her shoulders up.

"What?" He took another long drink. "This is good wine. What kind is it?"

Kenny picked up his glass and looked at it. "It's a red wine." He smiled.

Ed smirked.

Cindy picked up the bottle. "It's a Merlot. A Californian."

"It's good."

Kenny stretched his arms over his head, and his chest moved like something alive under his shirt.

"Jesus Christ, Kenny, did you ask the owner to bring cows into the gym so you'd have something to bench press?"

Kenny looked at his chest and his arms. "What?"

Ed shook his head. He took another sip of his wine. Different from beer, it worked its way through him like a massage. Still, he couldn't shake his heavy feelings.

Cindy looked toward the living room. "Danny was funny tonight. He was so good at his drawings."

"He's a good kid," Kenny said.

Ed nodded. Finishing his glass, he reached for the bottle and poured himself his fourth. "Get as much of him while you can," he said over the gurgling of the wine.

Cindy asked if he planned to leave soon.

"No," he said. "Not exactly." A June bug buzzed noisily against the screen, and Ed knocked it with the back of his hand. He told them what Susan had told him just a month before.

"France?"

Ed looked at his brother-in-law and nodded.

"Must have been a good opportunity," Cindy mused a moment later. "I don't see Susan just pulling up stakes if it wasn't a great opportunity."

Kenny nodded. "Not many kids get a chance like that."

Ed looked at both of them. "The hell with opportunity. The hell with 'a chance like that.' Tell me this. When am I supposed to see him? Where the hell do I fit into their plans?" He took a long drink of his wine.

Kenny and Cindy looked at the table.

"You know where I fit?" Ed continued. "Nowhere. Danny leaves in less than two months, and after that it could be years before I see him again. It's bullshit!"

Cindy shushed him and told him he was going to wake Danny.

He pointed across the table at Cindy. "She knew why I moved back and took that teaching job in Gwinn," he said in a lowered voice. "She knew I came back to be close to Danny—to be in his life. And she went and let this happen anyway."

Cindy touched her wine glass with her fingertips. "I don't think she did it to spite you."

"Well, she sure as hell didn't think about me when they made the decision."

"She didn't really have to," Kenny said.

Ed glared at him.

"And you can see him, right?" Cindy offered. "You can see him if you want."

Ed laughed. "Sure I can go see him. Let's see. Well, first I'll slap down a thousand bucks for the flight. Then I'll put down another thousand, at least, for a place to stay for a week. Then car rental. My meals. Paying for stuff to do with him..."

"Okay, I see."

"No, wait a minute. I think you have something there. I never thought of it. Hell, I can go see him once a month. I never thought to fly there."

"Okay, Ed," Kenny said.

Ed looked at him and then finished his wine.

Cindy cleared her throat. "Maybe they'll send him over here sometimes."

He breathed a derisive laugh through his nose. "Or maybe it would be cheaper if he and I met halfway. We could parachute into the ocean. Jesus Christ, Cindy. He's going to live in Paris! That will be where he lives. John's not going to drop down money every year so Danny can fly over and visit me."

"But why not? He's going to make good..."

"Good what? Good money. You can say it. Money. Well, fuck his good money. I don't need him to..."

Kenny stood up. "You're going to stop yelling in my house."

Ed looked up at his brother-in-law and sobered slightly.

"You've had too much wine and not enough food," Kenny continued. "Cind and I are going to go to bed, and you're not going to talk like that to her anymore. She may be your sister, but she's my wife, and you're not going to bark at her."

"Look," Ed said, "I'm sorry. You're right about the wine. I'm sorry. It's just that ... it's just everything."

"Good-night, Ed." Kenny guided Cindy towards the living room.

"Kenny," she said, "he's done. You're done, right Eddy? Let's just stay and..."

"No, Cind. No. In the morning we'll start over." He kept moving her toward the living room. "This is going nowhere good."

"I'll see you in the morning then, Eddy. Just go to bed. It will seem better in the morning."

The stairs barely squeaked for Cindy, but groaned under Kenny's massive frame.

Ed's heart slowed down. He looked at the screen and the bugs on it struggling to get to the light.

Sixteen

Ed lay in the darkness of his sister's guest room. He replayed the conversation from the kitchen in his head. Why did he have to get like that? Why did he have to be a hothead? Kenny had no patience for it. Ed guessed that the few people he did have in his life only tolerated him because of blood bonds.

He rolled on his side, flipped his pillow over, opened his window a little wider, but nothing made sleep come. It occurred to him that he must not be very likeable. Susan had always described him as sullen. Cindy called him moody. "You've got a way about you that isn't always easy," Sheila sometimes said. Where did it come from? Why couldn't he be more like the person he wanted to be? Why was he restless? He wanted only one thing, really. He wanted to be happy.

He would try, he decided. In the morning he would be agreeable. He'd help Cindy with the breakfast dishes and listen when she told him that he needed to be less sensitive. He'd go down to Kenny's work and apologize. He'd do whatever Danny wanted, and he'd stay and play games. He'd try to make this next week with his son a good week.

His son. In the guest room, separated from him, he imagined what it would be like to have him an ocean away. Holidays would be hell, but even the day-to-day stuff would get to him. What's Danny doing? Did the kid find anything that he stuck in his pocket? Did he have a cold? The questions would get no answers. Ed raised a fist in the air and then swung it down forcefully into the mattress. Alone. He would soon be absolutely alone. His son, the only one left who loved him unconditionally, would soon be gone. The next time he'd see him, he'd be some expatriate man. "Bon jour, Ed." Christ, the kid would probably call him Ed.

Cindy and Kenny's house knocked and pinged. Ed knew he had to use the bathroom before he fell asleep. Otherwise, he'd wake in the night and have to make his way groggily down the hallway, sleepy and lost.

After washing his hands, he made his way downstairs and into the living room. Somewhere in the walls of the house, the pipes worked to refill the toilet tank. Danny lay on the hide-a-bed, skinny arms and legs flailed out. He flopped restlessly. Ed found enough room and drew himself under the sheets. Rolling, he reached his left arm over his son and pulled him to him. Not waking, the boy flung an arm over Ed's chest and pulled his body in tight. He stopped fidgeting and settled into a deeper sleep. He made small sounds. His smooth, thin arm felt fragile, precious. His skinny fingers twitched slightly. Ed let his tears come.

In the morning, when he opened his eyes, Danny was gone.

Seventeen

Sunlight reflected off the thousands of strands of spider web in the branches above the Little Manistee River. It lit up like crystal, but I stepped as far as I could around it, imagining the size of the spider that made it.

"Smart spider," Uncle Kenny said. "How do they know to build their webs above the river where the insects swarm like they do?"

I shrugged and pushed some branches out of my way so I could continue downstream.

"Your dad could tell us," Kenny said. "Some built-in instinct, I'm sure."

The river moved quickly around our legs, but we had to pick our way slowly. A few bends back I'd been able to cast, but then the river narrowed and the overhang thickened.

Kenny started to sing. "Ludington, oh Ludington. I still hear your sea waves crashing."

I looked back at him, and he smiled.

"Sorry," he said. "You doing all right?"

I nodded. I didn't tell him about my mom or coyotes or wolves, but they'd been on my mind. He told me it wouldn't be too long before the river widened out again.

We kept working our way, but the river didn't widen.

"Let's take a break," he said. He pointed to a spot where we could get out and sit with our backs to some pine trees.

Sitting felt good. Uncle Kenny fished around in his pocket and then pulled out a cigarette. He put it in his mouth and then dug in the same pocket and came out with a match. "Don't tell your Aunt Cindy," he said before he struck the match. He set the flame to the cigarette. The cigarette bobbed in his mouth while he talked. "I gotta have a cigarette when I'm out fishing." He looked at me. "Our secret, right?"

I nodded.

We sat for a minute. He inhaled and then blew smoke that floated up into the pine boughs. Jimmy and I had shared a cigarette once, but we coughed so much that neither of us ever wanted another.

"So, you having fun?"

"Yeah," I said. I thought of something. "Nice walk in a river. Peaceful quiet. Concentration. This reminds me a lot of fishing, except of course without the fish." It was something John said the two times he took me on the Chocolay in Marquette and we got skunked.

Uncle Kenny laughed smoke out of his mouth. "Well, you little ... don't you worry. We'll get into some fish." He laughed again. "You gotta work for them sometimes. This river's going to widen out, and you'll get some fish on. It's early, yet. Don't you worry." He smoked for another couple of minutes and chuckled to himself.

A question had been eating at me for some time. "Why do people fall out of love?"

Kenny looked at me. His big neck spread out into big shoulders. "So, do you always ask the easy questions?"

I just looked at him.

He dug around and pulled out another cigarette. He lit it. He inhaled, and then smoke came out with his words. "Look," he said. "That one's not easy to answer. There's lots of reasons, I guess." He sucked on his cigarette again. "Is this about your folks?"

I nodded.

"Well, I know this much. They didn't fall out of love because of you."

I told him I knew. "They both told me that."

Uncle Kenny nodded. He took a few more drags on his cigarette. He told me he was going to tell me what he knew about love. "It's work," he said. "It's the hardest work you can get."

I looked at him.

He smiled and shrugged. "That's what I think," he said. "You meet somebody, and it feels so good and right that you get married. Then you start getting hit with stuff that you can't even imagine. It can make it really hard to stay in love because it doesn't always feel good and right all the time. Some people fall out of love, and some people work."

I thought about it. "So, my parents stopped working?"

Kenny's eyes squinted together for a minute, like he felt a slight pain. He took another drag on his cigarette. "It's not that easy," he said, talking out the smoke. "I think everyone wants to stay in love. The kind of work you have to do though is hard to learn. Really hard. If you don't learn it in time, things can fall apart. It's really nobody's fault. You can think you're working, but not be doing the right kind of work."

I looked at my fly patch and touched some of the flies on it. "I don't want to move to Paris."

"It's probably scary to think about," Kenny said.

I nodded. "I don't want to move away from everything."

"You're going to miss your dad, aren't you?"

I thought about it. "Yeah, that's part of it. I'll miss everything." He told me Dad was really going to miss me.

I shrugged. "I don't know," I said. "I think I make him mad. I don't know that he'll miss me much."

Kenny looked at me until I looked at him. "You're wrong," he said. "You're dead wrong. I know your dad. I know how he feels. He doesn't always show it right, but he's going to miss you until it hurts. It hurts him already. Don't ever think differently."

"Well, why does he always seem like he's mad? Why didn't we camp at St. Ignace like he said? Why aren't we going to Mackinac Island?"

Kenny rubbed the cigarette butt against the bottom of his boot. "He's just feeling bad is all. He doesn't want you to go. He's sad that you're going, and it will seem sometimes like he's mad at you."

It reminded me of what Dad had said about Jimmy. I nodded.

"Do you want to get in again? Do you want to fish?"

We worked our way again through the thick overhang. After another bend in the river, he asked me if I knew about the roll cast.

I shook my head.

"Well, you gotta learn the roll cast," he said. "There's fish in these tight spots in the river. Sometimes the biggest fish are here. You gotta know how to fish the tight spots and make them work for you."

He pulled line off his rod. He showed me the lift and loop of the roll cast. It was the first time he cast that day. Up until then he'd seemed happy with watching me.

Eighteen

Ed swallowed scrambled eggs along with his bitterness. Watching Cindy move around the kitchen, he tried to feel differently. He nodded slightly to himself and decided that there'd been no affront. Kenny took Danny fishing, nothing more. It was okay.

He stabbed up more eggs and chewed. He imagined them sneaking out of the house, and his anger returned. "You know, it wouldn't have hurt for them to at least try to wake me."

Cindy looked at him and then went back to turning a wash rag through a frying pan. "Do you even fly fish?" she asked.

"You don't need to fly fish to walk in a river. I have waders. I could have come along with them."

She set the frying pan into the rinse water and then sat at the table with Ed. "These were just little plans they cooked up while playing games last night. Kenny was excited that Danny fly fished. He took the morning off from work so he could take him. Danny was excited to go to a section of stream that was flies only. They were both excited. You should have seen them."

Ed picked through his eggs, working hard to drive his anger down inside him. He couldn't release it, but he could will himself into better feelings. "It's just that I only have these two weeks with him."

"Kenny knows that. He knows. They won't be gone all day." She stood again and went back to the sink. "I think this means a lot to Kenny to take him like this—just the two of them. His dad used to take him fly fishing. Kenny doesn't get a lot of chances to take a boy fishing."

Ed nodded. He went back to his eggs and pictured Kenny on the river with Danny. He didn't know enough about fly fishing to imagine what Kenny was saying, but he could feel what it felt like to tell a young man how to do something. There's nothing like a boy listening to you intently, as though something you have to say might be worth something. He nibbled at his lower lip. Kenny felt good, and Ed was happy for his brother-in-law. As long as they got back by noon.

Cindy asked him if he needed more eggs.

"No, thanks." He stood and walked his plate to the soapy water. Reaching in, he found the cloth and scrubbed. He dropped it in the rinse.

Cindy pulled the plate out and dried it. Reaching in, Ed found more dishes. He washed them. He and Cindy worked together.

"Where do you think you'll go next?"

Ed hadn't thought about it. "I don't know, really. I guess we'll head back up to St. Ignace and finish what we started. Camp. Check out Mackinac Island. I don't know."

With no more dishes to dry, Cindy flipped the towel onto her shoulder and moved to the coffee maker. She filled her cup. "You guys could stay here. Stay for a week. More if you want. We'd be happy to have you."

Ed took the towel from her shoulder and dried his hands. "That's a nice offer."

"I'm serious," she said. "It would be great. You'd have free food, a free place to stay."

"I've got money, Sis."

"I know, it's not ... I'm just saying that it would be great for you guys to stay. If the weather warms up, we could take Danny down to the lake to swim. We could pack a picnic."

He thought about it. He had nowhere else to be.

"I'd really like you to," she said. "I really would like to spend more time with Danny... I mean, not taking anything from you or anything. I mean, we could all spend time with him."

Ed admitted that Danny was having a good time, maybe the best time he'd had since the trip started.

"You see. I think he is too. It would be fun. For all of us."

Ed wasn't certain that it would be fun for him. He looked at the clock. "They should be home by noon. I mean, Kenny's got to go back to work, right?" he said. The feelings crept back—anger, resentment, abandonment. He poured another cup of coffee.

"Well, what do you think?" Cindy said. "Do you think you guys would want to stay for a week?"

He pushed his emotions down again. He nodded. "We could stay," he said.

Nineteen

Uncle Kenny told me to scan the ground for white. "Sometimes they're orange or bright yellow, but not as much anymore."

"Found another," he said. He picked up the golf ball from where it lay against a downed limb. It was white. Dropping it into his sack, he looked at me. "Now, you are opening your eyes, right?"

I smiled and nodded.

"Go on ahead of me. Get in front. That's why I'm finding them all. I'm in front."

I walked ahead. The ground around us was strewn with fallen branches and layers of dead leaves. Uncle Kenny told me we were in a ravine. I repeated the word. He said the ravine ran alongside one of the longest fairways, and golfers always sliced balls into it. "And," he said, "most of them are too damn lazy to get out of their carts and come down here and look for them."

"Why do you get them?"

He told me that when he was a kid he used to sell them for a quarter a piece. He'd shine the balls with a toothbrush and then display them in egg cartons. "I'd sit on a tee-off and when the golfers would come up, I'd ask them if they wanted to buy a ball. One summer I made two hundred bucks."

I stumbled along through the bottom of the ravine, and Uncle Kenny pointed out to me whenever I walked right past a ball.

"You really have to look," he said. "It can be right in front of your face, but if you're not careful you can go right past."

I asked if we were going to sell the ones we were finding.

"Nah. I golf myself, now. I'll throw these in my bag and then slice 'em into this same ravine. Maybe some kid will sell them back to me."

We were quiet for a time. I thought of Dad. This morning he seemed mad again when Uncle Kenny asked him to come hunt for golf balls with us. He said he was going to go for a walk. Fifteen minutes before we were about to leave, he came in smiling and said he would go. He said it would be fun.

Opening the passenger door, he stopped. "No," he almost whispered. "I don't need to go. You guys go. You take him, Kenny. That's your old stomping ground."

Kenny said he wanted all of us to go.

"No you don't," Dad sighed. "I don't blame you. You take him. You guys have fun." He started down the driveway.

"Come on, Ed," Uncle Kenny called. "Just come with us."

Without turning around, Dad waved us off. He hit the street and turned towards the beach.

I looked down. White. A golf ball. "Found one," I said, picking it up.

Kenny took it from me and examined it. "Pinnacle," he said. "They were considered the best ball when they first came out. Graceful as Titleist and tough as Top Flite."

A snapping noise moved through the treetops, arcing towards us. A golf ball cracked against the trunk behind Kenny, just a foot and a half over his head.

"Holy shit!" he shouted. He apologized. "That thing almost cracked my goddamn skull." "Sorry," he said again.

We stood still for a few seconds. Golfers hit their balls up on the fairway.

"Do you think we should leave?"

He looked at me. Then he looked around on the ground until he found the ball that hit the tree. He showed it to me. Pinnacle. "Hell no," he laughed. "We can't leave. They're just giving them to us now."

I laughed. We kept looking. Having found my first, I started seeing balls all over. Sometimes, walking, I'd kick them up from under the first layer of leaves. They were everywhere, and it was like egg hunting on Easter morning.

Twenty

The weather warmed. Ed sat on a towel on the beach with his arms hugged around his knees. Scooping up a handful of sand, he let it run out through his fist. Numb, as though he were floating in it, he stared silently at the cold water. Kenny and Cindy lay on a towel a few feet away.

Others were on the beach. There were umbrellas. Teenagers tossed a football around. Children dared the water and then ran away from its cold.

Danny walked with his head bent intently towards the sand. He dropped to his knees and picked through swatches of pebbles. Finding what he wanted, he ran to Kenny and Cindy to show them. Beach glass. Pieces of shattered bottles worn smooth by water and sand.

"Good one," Cindy said. "Show that one to your dad."

Danny looked at his father. Still kneeling, he held up the tiny shard between his finger and thumb. It looked as though he held nothing. Ed nodded and then watched his son run back down to the shore.

"Try to find a green one," Kenny shouted after him. "Or brown."

Ed watched his son. He couldn't see what the boy was picking up, but he saw the way he rolled it through his fingers and examined it before discarding or pocketing it. His face was intent, his body absorbed in the task. Behind him the lake loomed like every sadness yet to come, but the boy was lost. Lost in the best way. Lost as Ed had once lost himself in fishing. Lost as Ed had, for a time, lost himself in the firefighting.

Ed could not lose himself anymore, even now in the task of watching his son. Glancing at Cindy and Kenny, he imagined Susan and John on the beaches of southern France. Soon they would have Danny like this. Maybe he'd be discovering hermit crabs for the first time. He'd run from the shore to their blanket. The sand would be white. Pure. Absolving. It would give no reason to remember anything about Michigan. Lost in his new world, he wouldn't think of his father back in the States. John would be his father. His pere. Ed would be a vague memory.

"Loves the beach, doesn't he?" Kenny shouted.

Ed nodded, studying his brother-in-law's unnaturally developed body.

Cindy looked over. "Why don't you help him search?" she asked.

Ed looked at Danny. He shook his head. "He's doing fine. I think I'm going to go back up to the house, anyway."

Cindy shrugged. She and Kenny turned to watch Danny again.

Ed didn't want to so much, but he got to his feet, brushed off the sand, and carried out the gesture his words had promised.

"Eddy," Cindy called after him.

He didn't look back.

It was sand for a ways, and then long shoots of grass coming through the sand, and then just grass. When the sidewalk appeared, he followed it for a time until he spotted a city picnic table. He sat and looked back towards the beach.

The edge of town gave way to green, gave way to gold, gave way to the stretch of lake, which was not one color, but a range of hues changing with distance and depth. For a moment, the people had been dark lines and blotches on the sand, but in short time they moved.

The beach might well have been in southern France. Kenny and Cindy could be Susan and John. Danny would be Danny, but this would be the way Ed would imagine him from now on. Thin, a silhouette. He couldn't form the details—not the true details, not the changes that would come and slowly turn his son into someone he barely recognized. Ed imagined himself at ten (the pictures from his mother's shoebox), and he imagined himself at eighteen. Two totally different people. His son would grow into a stranger.

He stayed at the picnic table for a long time, only because he couldn't find the will to move. He stared out at the lake and the vague line of the horizon. He stayed, trying to feel and adjust to the sadness of his coming days.

In time, he looked for Danny, but the boy was gone. Kenny and

Cindy still lay on their towel. Was the boy looking for Ed? Did he want more time with his father? Ed looked back over his own path to see if his son was following.

A body rose from the water, and he knew it had to be Danny. Probably ran and dove on a dare from Kenny. He ran back towards shore, his legs kicking up great arcs of water. Reaching their towel, he fell between Kenny and Cindy.

Ed turned back towards the hazy, distant horizon.

Twenty-one

Ed set his beer on the bar.

"Take it easy, man," Kenny said. "It isn't a race."

Ed glanced at his brother-in-law. "I know it's not a race. It's just tasting good."

The bartender asked if Ed needed another.

"Just one more." The inside of his mouth tingled.

Kenny took a drink of his beer and then turned on his stool. When the bartender brought his new beer, Ed turned. A few locals were shooting a poor game of pool. Drink. Drink. Survey. Shoot. The balls rolled around and bounced off of each other but didn't go in the pockets. The men laughed and poked fun at each other's shots.

Ed asked if Kenny came to the bar very often.

"I don't go to any bar very often," he said, turning around.

Ed turned to the bar too. Both men drank quietly for a few minutes.

Kenny cleared his throat. "Cindy sure enjoys having Danny here. She really enjoys spending time with him."

Ed nodded.

Kenny said that he was glad that they stayed. "It's been some time since I've seen Cind this happy."

"Didn't really have anywhere else we needed to be."

The men drank again.

Ed set another empty draft glass on the bar a moment later. "You know," he said. "I try and try, but I just can't figure out how in hell things got so fucked up."

Kenny took a long drink.

"I went from having a job that I liked, a wife, and a kid to having no wife, no kid, and a job I can't stand. How the hell does that happen?"

Kenny said he didn't know.

The cue ball cracked into the others.

"The balls ain't supposed to still be in a triangle after you break," one of the pool players teased.

Ed's jaw felt loose. He could say anything. "I really tried to make the marriage work. I made sacrifices like they say you'll have to. I changed. What the fuck did she want?"

"Take it easy, Ed."

"I am taking it easy. I'm talking to you. We're talking, right? Can't I talk? Cindy told us to go out and talk."

Kenny put his big hand on Ed's shoulder. "Of course we can talk. But you're not talking, you're barking."

"Sorry. I didn't mean ... I'm not barking. I'm just saying that I can't put my finger on how I got to this point. I'm spending what will probably be the last two weeks I'll spend with my son. How do you get to this point?"

The bartender came over. Kenny tried to wave him off.

"Come on, man. Don't. I want another beer. I'm fine. I'm a grown man. I can get another beer. I know when to say no."

Kenny shrugged.

Ed pushed his glass forward. "One more," he said.

Kenny finished his beer.

"And one more for my brother-in-law," Ed shouted down towards the bartender.

Kenny shook his head. "No, I'm good. Two's my limit."

"Your limit? Come on. What are you, some kind... Just let me buy you a beer. It's my treat."

"No," he said. He looked towards the bartender who was looking his way, one hand on a tap handle. "No," he said.

The bartender nodded.

"Fine, I'll drink alone. I'm getting used to doing things alone."

Kenny exhaled loudly. "That's your own damn fault."

"What?" Ed pushed a dollar towards the bartender, who put a beer in front of him.

"Nothing."

"No. You said something. You said everything that's happening is my fault."

"How many times can you sink the goddamn eight ball?" one of the pool players shouted, laughing. "This is getting to be a waste of quarters."

The other player said they should keep playing anyway. "Fuck the eight ball. Right?"

They kept playing.

Kenny rolled his beer glass between his hands.

"Well," Ed said. "What did you mean? I want to hear how this is my fault."

"Nothing. It was nothing. I'm talking out of my ass."

"What? Do you think it's my fault because I quit my job with the DNR for her? I knew she hated how I had to go out in the field—how I'd be gone for weeks sometimes. I knew she didn't like it. So, I got my teaching certificate. I went from a dream job to a nightmare for her. Is that how this is my fault?"

Kenny shrugged. "Nope. You're right. None of this is your fault. Everywhere something went wrong, Susan is behind it."

"Come on, Kenny. The hell with that. If you've got something to say, then say it."

He stopped rolling his glass. He turned on his stool and faced Ed. "You want to know what I think? Okay. You're a jumper. Something goes wrong or looks wrong, you jump. You don't look. You don't talk. You jump."

"What do you..."

"Just look at the facts, Ed. When your marriage was getting rocky, you assumed it was your job. You went back to school, got a new job, and just made things worse. When your marriage finally did fall apart, you took off for California. You weren't around for any custody hearings. You lost Danny. Then you start something good with Sheila, which on a whim you throw away to move back to Marquette. You're a jumper."

Ed felt sucker punched. It was a punch he deserved.

"Look, I'm sorry to be so blunt. Sometimes I just don't..."

Ed shook his head. "No, you're right. Everything you just said is true. Holy shit. It's like you held up a mirror, and I finally saw myself for the dumbass I am."

Kenny patted him on the back. "Come on, now." He called the bartender down and ordered another beer. "Hell, I'll make three my limit tonight. Right? I shouldn't have said anything. Cind says I'm always shooting my mouth off."

A numb haze washed over Ed. He stared ahead into the bottles lined along the back of the bar. An hour could have passed. He didn't know.

Kenny nudged him. "Hey, those guys are done. Let's play a game of pool. Let's move around a little." He held up a dollar and asked the bartender for quarters.

Ed's break scattered the balls wildly, but when they stopped moving, none had dropped into a pocket. He could feel that he was drunk.

"Nice break," Kenny said. He circled the table. "Think I'll take the solids," he announced. He sank a few and then scratched. "You're up."

Ed slumped into a nearby chair. "I don't want to finish. I don't want to play."

Kenny walked over and loomed above him. "You have to play. We paid. Come on, just finish the game."

"I can't play pool right now," he sighed. He ran his fingers through his hair and stared at the ground. "I lose him. In less than two weeks, I won't see him again. What do I do then? I've got nothing."

Kenny sat down. He sighed. "Want me to tell you what I figured out? You do? Good. I figured out you have to do something. You grab for something that makes sense, and you do it."

Ed looked at him. "What should I do? Start weight lifting?"

"It saved my ass."

"No, thanks."

"Whatever. I'm not even saying weight lifting is what you should do. But you have to do something. I know about hurting. Cind and I almost didn't make it. Then I decided that I wanted to make it. We both did, but kind of on our own. You have to decide you're going to do something. That's the only way it works."

"And what if you don't?"

Kenny shrugged. "I don't know. You slip away. You're living, but not really. I mean, I wasn't too far from it. Both Cind and I."

"Over not having kids?"

Kenny nodded.

"Tough, huh?"

"Toughest thing I've ever been through."

Ed rubbed his eyes. "What I never understood was why you guys didn't adopt."

"We would have. We tried." With one hand Kenny massaged the tricep of his other arm. "Look, since we're being so honest tonight, let's just say that my record's not clean. I did stupid things before I met Cind. It stays with you."

Ed asked what Kenny had done.

"Never mind. I've already told you more than I would have liked. Just keep working on your beer, and maybe you'll forget I even told you." He stood up. "Come on, let's keep playing."

Ed took a sip of his beer and set the empty glass on the table. "This would all be a lot easier if she hadn't married that asshole, John."

Kenny took a shot and sank a solid. "He doesn't seem so bad to me. That's a consolation, right? That at least she married someone who's good to her and your son."

Something burned through Ed. "The hell it's a consolation. And how the hell would you know that he's not so bad."

Kenny stood from stooping over the table. "Because they stayed with us for a week last summer."

Ed swallowed. "What? My ex-wife and her new husband stayed with you guys? They slept in the same goddamn bed I'm sleeping in?" He stood up and bumped the table. His beer glass fell over and then rolled off the side where it smashed on the floor.

"Hey!" the bartender shouted. "What the hell."

"Take it easy, Ed. You know Susan and Cind are good friends. You know..."

"No, no, no. When you divorce someone you lose everything. You don't get to keep the sister-in-law as a friend. I mean, she's got to lose something too, right? I mean... How the hell did it come together that they stayed with you guys?"

Kenny said it was something Cindy and Susan worked out. "You were in California. You had a new woman. What does it matter?"

Ed laughed. "What does it... I bet you assholes had a pretty good time raking ol' Ed over the coals, didn't you? You sonuva..." He moved forward and shoved his hands into Kenny's massive chest.

Kenny stepped back and caught himself. "Ed, god damn it."

"My ex-wife. My fucking ex..." He threw a wild punch and caught Kenny in the cheek.

"God damn it." Kenny hugged his arms around Ed and wrestled him to the floor. "Now would you just take it easy. Don't do this."

"She's gotta lose something, too!" The side of Ed's face rubbed savagely into the floor as he tried to free himself from Kenny's grip.

The bartender shouted that the police were on their way.

"We gotta get out of here. I don't need police." Kenny lifted Ed's face and then rapped it again against the floor. "I don't fucking need police, Ed."

"Alright. Alright. Just let me up."

"We gotta get out of here. So no more."

"Alright. Just let me up."

Kenny loosened his grip. Ed scrambled to his feet and bolted for the darkness through the threshold of the open door. Running, he had a vague idea in his mind. Beach. He'd run to the beach. He'd wait. He looked around, waited for police lights, but the street remained dead.

Panting, slowing to a walk, he had a thought. It was more a dread realization. He was wasting the last bit of time he had with his son. He'd already pissed away a week. A week left. One week. He needed a plan. Like Kenny said, he needed to do something.

He stumbled down onto the sand. The endless black of the lake spread before him. Akin to a whisper, the waves broke at the shore-line. He listened.

Twenty-two

I opened my eyes to the darkness. Something woke me.

"Danny? Are you up?"

My eyes adjusted. Dad sat on the edge of my bed. He was a shadow.

"Danny?"

"I'm up," I told him.

He told me to get out of bed. He told me I didn't have to get dressed. I could sleep in the van.

"What time is it?"

"It doesn't matter," he said, standing up. "Just get up. I packed up your stuff. Do you want me to carry you? I can carry you to the van." His voice was different. Excited.

I asked him why we were leaving.

"I had an idea. We're wasting time here. We have to get going."

I could see more in the room. My little duffle bag was on the floor next to his.

"Where are we going?" I sat up.

A noise came from upstairs. Dad looked up. Some time passed before he looked down and answered my question. "Montana."

"Montana?" It was out west. I knew that. Somewhere in the middle? I wasn't sure.

He nodded. "Yeah! I figured out what we could do." He told me there was a trout I could catch in Montana that I couldn't catch in Michigan. "It's not a Grayling," he said.

"What is it?" I found my shoes and slipped them on.

"Cutthroat trout," he said.

"Cutthroat," I said, tying my laces. I liked the word in my mouth. I looked up. "Why are we leaving now? What time is it?"

He picked up the duffle bags and told me it was late. "I already said goodbye to Uncle Kenny and Aunt Cindy. They know we have to leave now."

"Why?" I asked.

"We have to catch the ferry. There's a car ferry that will take us across Lake Michigan into Wisconsin. The SS Badger."

"Badger?"

He smiled, nodding.

He started towards the door and I followed. He stopped and turned around to me. "Do you want to do this? Do you want to go try and catch a cutthroat? We can stay if you really want to stay. I just thought this would be something just for us."

I would miss Uncle Kenny and Aunt Cindy, but I wanted to ride the car ferry. And I wanted to fish in Montana like the guys in the programs that John and I watched on Saturday mornings. "I want to go," I said.

He smiled and messed my hair. "Good," he said. He opened the front door slowly. The darkness was different from any other time. It was so quiet. Dad and I could have been the only people alive.

"Don't slam your door," he said when we got to the van.

We drove through town. There were no other cars or people. We headed toward the darkness of the lake. We parked.

"Where's the ferry?" I asked.

He told me it wasn't in from Manitowoc yet. He smiled and told me to sleep.

"Why did we have to leave so early if it's not here yet? When will it get here?"

"Just go to sleep," he said. "You can sleep in back."

I climbed in the cot. I could feel that it would take a long time to sleep. Mom came into my head. I missed her. I tried not to cry. I remembered that the divorce was her fault. I didn't cry.

I heard paper in the front seat. Dad flipped through a book of maps.

Twenty-three

The dark blue of the lake met the light blue of the sky forming a crisp line of horizon. Dad and I leaned against the front rail. "Takes about four hours to cross," he said.

A cold morning wind stung our faces. The blue lounging chairs around the deck were all empty. "It's really cold," I said, speaking up above the roar of the boat pushing through the water.

"It's not cold," Dad said. "It's refreshing."

I looked at him, but he was staring out toward the horizon as though there were something to see. "I don't know. I think it's pretty cold," I argued. I was hungry too but I didn't tell him.

He stared ahead.

I asked him what happened to his cheek.

"What?" He touched the reddish-blue spot. "This? Nothing. Walked into a wall while packing up in the dark last night."

I thought of him packing while I was still asleep. "How long do you think it will take us to get to Montana?"

He looked at me. "I don't know for sure. A good two solid days of driving. Maybe more. You up for it?"

I nodded. He put his hand on my shoulder, and we looked out toward the water.

I asked him if he'd ever caught a cutthroat trout.

He shook his head. "Nope. I've only fished Michigan. This will be a treat. You and I fishing a brand new fish together. The ol' cutthroat." He squeezed my shoulder.

"What do they look like?"

"I don't know for sure. I know they have red slash marks on their lower jaw. It's why they call them cutthroat."

I nodded.

"This is going to be fun, isn't it? Just you and me. I've never been to Montana before. Or Minnesota or North Dakota for that matter."

I looked behind us at the tip of the ship's red smokestack. "I've never been out of Michigan before," I said.

Dad took his hand off my shoulder and looked out towards the horizon again. "Well, you'll be out of Michigan soon enough. France is pretty big time out of Michigan."

I looked out at the water. I didn't want to think about France or how much I was going to miss Jimmy. I wondered how long it would be before I'd have a friend in France. Something worked at my eyes, and I had to buckle my lips in against my teeth to keep from crying.

Dad crouched down next to me. He looked at me. "You okay?"

I nodded.

"You still want to go, right? After those cutthroat?"

"Yeah."

He exhaled. He started to stand, but then crouched again. "I'm not telling you what I'm going to tell you for any reason other than I think you should know," he said.

I didn't know what he was talking about. A man came out onto the deck, shivered, and then turned back inside. The tops of my ears were stinging.

Dad looked into my face. "When you move away, it will probably be a long time before I see you."

I sniffed and swallowed. "What do you mean? How long?"

"Look, I'm not trying to say this to ... it's just that I think we should know that this next week together needs to be special. It just could be some time before..."

"How long?" I knew by the way he was talking that it would be a long time.

"I don't know for sure, Danny. It could be years I guess. I mean, I'll try to get over next year, but after that it could be... It could be a long time."

Tears ran hotly down my cheeks. "Why?" My voice sounded funny.

"It just comes down to money. I don't make the money John makes. I can't afford just to fly over to France. It's expensive. Maybe I could afford it every five years. I don't know, maybe three." Dad wiped at my tears with his big thumbs.

"I don't want to move!"

Dad hugged me to him. I couldn't stop crying.

He told me to stop crying. He told me everything would be

okay. He told me that we would talk on the phone.

I talked into his shoulder. My words were broke up with sobbing. "I don't want to talk on the phone. I just want to stay here in Michigan. I want things to stay like they are. I want to see Jimmy. I want to see you. Why did Mom have to fall out of love?"

Dad held me tight, but then pushed me back after a time, holding me at arm's length. His shoulder was wet where my face had been.

"Look," he said, "we've got this week left together. Let's make the most of it. Then, with everything else, we'll wait and see. Maybe it won't be as bad as we think."

"I ... don't ... want ... to ... move."

Dad chuckled a little. "Stop now. Don't cry anymore. I can barely understand what you're saying. It won't be so bad. Let's just... Are you hungry? We can go in and eat. I saw the way you were looking at that arcade when we got on board. Want to shoot down some space invaders after breakfast?"

I looked at him. "Space invaders?"

"Yeah, isn't that what you kids like? Or maybe it's the Pac-Man you want to play."

I giggled. "Those games are ancient." A final sob shook me.

He stood up and walked me towards the door. "Well, any game is radical by me," he said. "I'm hip. I'm on the down low."

"Dad." I felt better for a minute, but then he stopped joking around, and I felt bad again. Unless I fought it, I would cry. Dad seemed the happiest he'd been in some time.

He turned on the stairs and poked me in the stomach. "Come on yah scurvy swine. Let's get down to the galley for some grub and rum."

Twenty-four

Ed Winters stood in the open doorway of a motel about thirty miles outside of St. Paul. He touched his cheek, still raw from where Kenny had rapped it against the bar floor. The night was dark, and the cool air felt good. It was quiet, even with the intermittent passing cars. Approaching headlights, the car itself, taillights. He watched and wondered where the night could be taking them.

The miles he'd put behind them today were flat. First the flat and then later hills rolling into hills—all lonely country. It was a road for too much thinking, arguing with oneself. There'd been some sense of change around Green Bay, some sense of city, but every mile before it and each after was equally desolate. The red barns and silos, the two things he wanted to see, were always far away from the highway, on the edges of acres and acres of field. It was a sad, lonely stretch of blacktop. He imagined it as his life without Danny, without anything, that lay ahead.

Danny was behind him in one of the beds, rolling restlessly. He'd slept on and off through most of the drive. Ed had felt exhausted through the trip, but sleep wouldn't come here in the motel. He stood in the doorway in only his boxer shorts.

"Danny, you up?"

No answer.

Another car approached, its noise growing in volume and then doppling down as it passed. Beyond the highway lay darkness for miles. Distant lights shone vague and dim.

He pushed his fingers through his damp hair. He told himself they were going fishing. He was taking the boy, his son, to Montana to fish. He wanted to leave the boy with something to remember.

He did the math. Two more days of driving. They'd have to find a river. And then? One day of fishing. Two if they pushed it. Then the race back across the northernmost highways of America to get Danny back just under the deadline.

No. Fuck her. She could give him an extra day. An extra week even. Danny was his son—the only piece of meaning he had in the world. She had John and money and Paris. John would want his own kids. They could have their own fucking kids.

He looked back at Danny moving under the sheets.

"You up?"

Nothing.

Ed put his hand on the doorknob. He pictured Susan and John on a Ludington beach with Kenny and Cindy.

Fuck her. She had everything. He had nothing. He wasn't coming back. They'd have to come after him if they wanted Danny.

Twenty-five

Dad stood in the doorway framed in a bluish light. He was a shadow. A shadow in its underwear. He scratched his thick belly. A car went by, and then I heard nothing except his mumbling.

Today on the drive he told me what he did as a fisheries biologist for the DNR. It was really boring. Almost as boring as the drive. I pretended to sleep, and sometimes I fell asleep. The next day our drive would be even longer.

Dad said my name and asked if I was awake.

I didn't answer. I didn't want to talk.

Another car went by.

He ran his fingers through his hair and slumped against the door frame. He was fatter than John. He shrugged his hands into the air. He did it again. Then he was still.

A moment later he punched a fist into his other hand. I jumped.

He asked me again if I was awake. His voice was different, edgy.

He held the doorknob for a moment and stared out. He spit. He closed the door, and the room went black. I didn't like being alone in the darkness with him.

He got into his own bed. "Fuck her," he mumbled.

Fuck. I said the word quietly to myself. A whisper of a whisper. I'd never heard a grown up say the word except in movies. I was afraid, but I wasn't sure why.

Twenty-six

Ed stood near the bank. The shallows of the upper Madison moved around his ankles. Danny stood farther out, thigh deep, casting to likely spots. Even after three days his accuracy still needed work. This was bigger water than almost anything in Michigan. Trout were rising, but he couldn't get his fly to them. By the time he did, he'd slapped the surface too many times, and the fish were spooked. Ed wanted to yell advice, but he didn't know any.

"Just keep trying," he finally shouted. "Don't get frustrated." Ed never felt lost in the outdoors. It frustrated him. But then what did he know about any of this? Montana. Its skies eerie and endless, something like falling forward with nothing to catch yourself. The Rockies always on the horizon like a mirage. Rivers as disconcerting and wide as five-lane highways. Fly fishing? What did he know?

He knew Montana had cutthroat trout. The name had stuck with him. And, he knew about the Madison River. A friend of his in the DNR had fished it. He'd said it was a good river. Probably not the best reason to drag his son across three states.

Driving had taken four hours longer than he would have guessed to get to Three Forks—the confluence site of the Madison, Jefferson, and Gallatin rivers. They hit a fly shop as soon as they set up camp. A smug man in his twenties had told them the flies they would need: Bitch Creek nymphs, girdle bugs, yuk bugs, parachute Adams, sofa pillows, Bird's stoneflies, elk hair caddis, royal wulffs, and marabou streamers. "Crazy names, eh?" Ed said, poking his son. Danny looked serious. Looking Ed and Danny over, the man recommended a guide. He recommended fishing the upper Madison, another sixty miles south. Ed shook his head to both. Guide? He didn't want another man around. He'd had enough of that with Kenny. Another sixty miles? Hell, no.

They fished the lower Madison for two days. Access wasn't always easy. They drove all over, but something always kept them from the water. They finally found a way in below the mouth of Beartrap Canyon, but there was walking involved. Danny complained that they weren't fishing. When they did finally get in, he complained that there weren't fish. Fish eventually started rising to his fly, but no cutthroat. He caught some smaller rainbows, even one they were able to cook up. In the evening he had larger fish on, browns Ed guessed, but the boy always lost them. Frustrated, Danny was often close to tears. "Come on, Danny," Ed consoled. "They're just fish."

"But that's why we're here," the boy countered.

The first night they drove back to Three Forks. In the morning, they moved their camp closer to Beartrap Canyon.

The best part of the trip so far had been the makeshift dump they'd stumbled across along one of the two-track roads. Danny found a rare bottle. He told Ed about having to get rid of the collection. "No," Ed said. "The hell with what John says. I'll keep the bottles for you."

Danny called to Ed, snapping him from his reverie.

"What?"

"I can't get 'em," Danny shouted over the rush of river noise. "They just won't hit my fly." His voice wavered.

Ed told him again to keep trying.

Having studied maps for the past two nights, he knew the ranges around them. To the west, the high peaks of the Madison Range. To the east, the tree-covered slopes of the Gravelly Range. The river itself was the "fifty-mile riffle" it was described as in the brochures. It was beautiful water. Beautiful country.

But if he thought too much, nothing seemed beautiful.

The next day he was supposed to be in Marquette, supposed to bring Danny back to Susan. He wasn't sure if he'd resolved himself to his decision, but he couldn't be back in Michigan in one day. He'd have to call her. Driving across the state, the gaping sky of Montana had made him jittery, doubtful. On the river, watching his son, he felt different, secure. The ranges flanked them. The river did not seem as wide. The boy was getting strikes. He guessed that he could do it. He could just take him. Couldn't he?

Looking around he tried to lose himself in this beauty he'd never known—the beauty of a new state—a big state—like the beauty of the Pacific he'd found in California. He tried to lose himself. He looked around. After a moment, he only felt lost.

Danny waded back to him. "I don't want to fish anymore."

"What? You're not having fun?"

"I'm just sick of fishing."

Ed asked him if he wanted to get some lunch and then come back.

He shook his head. "I just don't want to fish anymore."

"But you didn't get a cutthroat."

He said he didn't care. They started back towards the van.

Ed put his arm around his son and pulled him to him as they walked. "Do you think we should have hired a guide?"

The boy shrugged. "The guy said he thought we needed one."

Twenty-seven

It was Monday in Three Forks, Montana. It was Monday in Marquette, Michigan. Ed Winters huddled into a pay phone outside of a downtown building. The downtown itself was small and dead. Maybe two thousand people lived in Three Forks. A few trucks rolled past, the drivers with stubble and cowboy hats.

A family eventually went by him as he read the directions for his calling card. They appeared to be tourists. The father wore a New York Yankees hat. He tried to excite his children by mentioning the Lewis and Clark caverns. The children remained bored-looking.

Lewis and Clark's names were all over Three Forks. The explorers had camped for two summers not too far away at the headwaters of the Missouri River. Sacagawea herself had been kidnapped as a young girl not very far from what would later be Three Forks. This was long before she'd ever been a part of the Lewis and Clark expedition. Ed had been reading the place mats in local restaurants. He knew more than he'd ever wanted about the area. He held the phone, but didn't dial.

Danny's silhouette sat in the passenger seat of the van. He looked so small with just his head and neck above the dashboard. Ed didn't know what he was doing. He still didn't know what he'd say to his ex-wife. He pushed his fingers through his hair. This was kidnapping if he did it. It was still something if he didn't. He was in Montana on the last day of the two weeks.

The phone rang. Susan picked up.

"It's me. It's Ed." His heart beat furiously.

"When are you bringing him home?"

"Hello to you, too."

She asked him again when he was bringing Danny home.

He said he didn't know.

"Well, have him here by noon. We have a lot to do."

He swallowed. He told her he couldn't have him there by noon.

"Ed, what do you... Why not? I don't understand."

"We're not back in Gwinn, yet."

She asked where they were. "You're not still in St. Igance, are you?"

He told her they weren't.

"Then where are you?"

A local sheriff's cruiser went by. The driver studied Ed. Ed felt a rush of something go through him. The car kept going.

"Tell me where you are," Susan said tersely.

"We're in Montana. He wanted to go fishing," he started to explain. "He wanted to fish some big water. We just lost track of the time."

She told him to tell her he was joking.

He shook his head. "I'm not joking. We're in Montana. We're…"

"You go to an airport right now," she interrupted. "You get on a plane, and you get my son home to me. Now. I don't even want to know how you ended up in Montana. You stupid asshole, you get him home."

"Nice mouth for a doctor's wife."

"Get him home, Ed."

"It's not that easy."

"You're going to make it *that easy*. Nothing is ever easy with you, but you're going to make this as easy as possible. You're going to fly my son home. You're going to pay for the tickets. You're going to do whatever you have to do to get your van home. I don't care. This is your fault, and you're going to fix it. I want him home. I *want* him home, Ed. I really don't give a damn how much it costs you."

"I'm sure you don't."

Susan exhaled. She talked calmly. "I'm not interested in whatever you're trying to start. I don't want it, Ed. I don't want it. You're in Montana with my son. By tomorrow you'll be in Michigan. It's simple. It's easy. You'll figure out a way. I want my son here with me now. I'm not interested in playing 'Eddy's the victim here.' I've played it. I won't play it."

Eddy. His sister's name for him. Susan's derogatory name for him. Whatever had been rushing through him turned bitter. "I'm not asking you to play anything. I'm telling you we are in Montana.

We're in Three Forks, Montana. There's not a helluva a lot of flights out of Three Forks to Marquette."

She said she didn't care how many layovers he had. "You get him home! We have to pack. We have a huge garage sale."

"He doesn't want to get rid of his bottles."

"What ... Ed. Just get on a plane—"

"We're not flying. We're not getting on a plane today. You can stop talking about it," he said decisively.

She was quiet. "What are you telling me? Then when are you going to have him home? I don't understand this. When will he be home?" Her voice was quieter, tinted with confusion. Her voice recognized that he held the cards.

"I'm not sure. I'm not sure I'm going to bring him home. I'm keeping him."

"What?"

"Pretty rotten feeling, isn't it?"

"What the hell does that mean, Ed? What does that mean?"

"It means what it means." He hung up. He couldn't talk to her anymore. He couldn't take what was coming. Everything she'd say would be right, and he didn't want it screamed at him. He wanted to be somewhere where somebody thought he was right. He wanted someone to say, "He's your son, too. France isn't fair. Custody or no custody. After you just moved back to be with him, France just isn't fair. You did what you had to do. I'm sure other people would do what you're doing."

He turned towards the van.

Twenty-eight

Coming across the parking lot, Dad looked lost, dazed. He moved in the direction of the van, but not exactly towards it. He scratched his fingers into his hair. I hoped he wasn't thinking of another river we could fish. I was tired of fishing. I was tired.

He finally looked up, saw the van, saw me, and then started a little jog to the driver's side door. He hopped up onto the seat and looked at me.

"You okay?"

I nodded. "I'm just really tired."

"You didn't sleep good last night?"

I shrugged. "I think I slept pretty good."

He told me I could get some sleep on the road.

"Where are we going? I don't want to fish anymore."

He chuckled. "Don't worry. No more fishing." He rubbed his palms on his thighs. "I just got off the phone with your mom."

I looked over at him. I felt a little like I could throw up. Then it went away.

"I asked her for another week. I thought we could use another week together. If you want, she said okay."

I missed Jimmy. I wanted to have some time with him before we left for Paris, before I would never see him again. I wanted to spend time with Dad, too. He'd been fun in Montana. He seemed happier. "What will we do?" I asked. Something at the mention of her made me want to see Mom, too. I missed her.

He shrugged his fingers above the steering wheel. "If you wanted, I was thinking Disneyland. It's not far at all from where I lived in Pomona. We could go to the ocean, too. There's a lot we could do. I could show you some things."

Something rushed through me. I didn't feel tired. "Disneyland?!"

He nodded and smiled. "I think we need a little vacation from all this fishing."

I laughed. I nodded, too. I hadn't felt so happy and excited in a long time.

"You ever been to Disneyland or Disney World?" Dad asked.

I shook my head. "I went to Great America. That was with you and Mom."

Dad nodded slowly. "I remember."

I rubbed my hands together and then clapped. "Let's go."

"I want to be sure you're up for this. We'll have a couple nine-hour days on the road. You up for more driving?"

"I'm up for Disneyland," I said.

Dad nodded. He started the van.

Feeling tired again, I reclined my seat back. I felt a chill and shivered it off. "Wake me up when we get to Disneyland."

Some time passed. I looked over. Dad, both hands on the wheel, stared out through the windshield at the empty parking lot. He looked lost. I remembered him looking the same way when I woke up and peeked at him while we were driving through North Dakota. He called it the Badlands. I liked that. "Can't believe I drove through this on purpose," he'd said. He'd looked tired, but more than just tired. He'd looked scared.

"Dad?"

He shook his head slightly. His face changed. "Yeah, okay," he said. He shifted into drive.

Twenty-nine

Something woke Ed Winters. Idaho Falls. It was the first thought in his head. He guessed they would have come farther, maybe even into northern Nevada. But, the Rockies. Beautiful at a distance, but hell to drive through. It wasn't the highest elevations, but it was enough. It was white knuckle driving for a man who'd seldom been out of Michigan.

The sound came again.

His son was mumbling, talking in his sleep. Dreaming, Ed guessed. "Danny?" What nightmare could be holding him, shaking him in its terror? Could he sense something? Did he feel the void his father was driving them in to? Here, in this Idaho motel, hundreds of miles from anywhere he knew, in the darkness of wide country and closed curtains, Ed realized the nightmare of what he was doing. Stealing his son. Taking him towards nothing. Having nothing for him except a father's haggard love.

More frenzied mumbling.

"Danny?" Ed rolled out of the covers and to the other bed. "Wake up, son. You're having a nightmare." Reaching, he felt the heat before he found the boy.

Fever.

No. It couldn't be. With a practiced hand, he found the small forehead in the darkness.

Burning up. How high? Ed didn't know.

"No ... I don't want ... no..."

Ed stroked his palm over his son's damp hair. "Danny?"

"What? ... no. No."

Ed took his son's shoulders, tried to prop him higher on the pillow. "Come on, Danny. You need to wake up. You have a fever."

"Dad, no. I just want to sleep. I'm tired. I just want to sleep."

Ed felt the forehead again. It felt like a small radiator under his hand. "Danny, I just want you to have something to drink. Just wake up for a minute." He remembered something about high fevers being bad in children. But what did bad mean? Susan would know.

More mumbling. Whimpering.

Ed left the bed. He walked slowly forward waving his hand in front of him through the darkness. He unwrapped a small plastic cup from the bathroom and filled it with water. Opening the curtain on the way back to the bed, he let a little moonlight into the room. His heart beat in his throat.

"Danny?"

The boy was sleeping, making small noises. Ed set the water on the nightstand and went back to the bathroom. He ran a washcloth under the tap.

"Dad ... don't." Danny shifted and kicked the covers off. He reached up and took the washcloth from his forehead.

Ed put it back. "Just keep it there. It will cool you down."

"I am cool. I'm cold." He squirmed.

Ed pulled the covers back over his son. "Are you up enough now to drink some water? You should drink." He reached the glass and touched it to his son's lips.

Danny pushed it away and water spilled on the bed.

"Danny."

"I don't want a drink." He pulled the washcloth off again.

Ed squeezed his own forehead. "You need to take care of this. You have a fever."

"Just let me sleep." He moved twitchingly.

Ed told him he wasn't sleeping. "You're restless. You're not getting sleep."

"Just let me sleep."

Ed put the washcloth back, but he knocked it away again.

He exhaled. "Do you want anything? I can go out and get some medicine. It would bring the fever down so you sleep better."

Nothing. The boy had fallen into a fidgeting sleep again. Ed watched him, but nothing changed after ten minutes. The mumbling didn't return.

Sighing, he crawled back into his own bed. Sleep wouldn't come, but he would rest and listen. He was doing this. He was stealing his son. His son had a high fever.

He stared up into the gray darkness.

Thirty

Ed woke to Danny's bawling.

"I want mom!"

"What? What, Danny?" Fever. Idaho Falls. Stealing his son. His mind clicked the tragic puzzle pieces together.

"I want Mom!"

"What's wrong? What's the matter?" He went to his son's bed. The clock glowed on the nightstand. Two in the morning. They'd slept for an hour.

"I want Mommy! I'm sick! I'm sick!"

"What's wrong? Did you throw up? What's wrong?" He found the bedside lamp and snapped its light into the room.

"No. No." Danny started sobbing. "I want Mommy. I want Mommy." His small body writhed in half-sleep.

"Just tell me what's wrong," Ed pleaded. "Here, drink some of this water."

"No!" the boy shrieked in what amounted to a tantrum.

"Jesus Christ, Danny. What the hell is wrong?" Ed was near shouting himself. He put his hand on his son's forehead again. He couldn't be sure, but it felt as though the temperature had gone up.

Danny knocked his hand away. "I want Mommy. I want Mommy." His hair looked as though it'd just been towel dried after a bath.

Ed scooped up the small furnace of his son's body and held him to his chest. "Mommy isn't here. I'm here. I'm here. What do you want?" Ed's own tears weren't far away.

Danny pushed and struggled. "No. No. No. I want Mommy. I want Mommy. Where's Mommy?"

"She's not here. I'm here. Daddy's here." He held the boy to him tightly. "I'm here."

"No," the boy shrieked.

Someone moved in the room next door.

Ed tried to shush him. "Settle down, now. It's okay. I can get you what you want."

"I want Mom," the boy sobbed. "I want Mommy." And then he

sobbed more and didn't speak again. His sobbing idled down.

Ed held him, rocked him, his own body sweating from the heat of his son's.

"Will you drink some water, now?" He held the cup to the boy's lips. Danny drank it all. "There you go. Do you want more?"

He nodded weakly.

Ed nearly sprinted to the bathroom. He let the water run. He flushed the toilet to try to make it colder.

Danny finished it.

Ed asked if he wanted more.

He shook his head. He sniffled.

"What about TV? Do you want to watch a show? I can try to find something."

"Yeah."

"You do?" He leapt to the television, moving quickly before something broke the spell that held his son in something close to calm.

The television glowed into the room and brought the calm, relaxed, laughing voices of a late night talk show. It was after Leno and Letterman. Ed recognized neither the host nor the guest, but he didn't care. He welcomed them like family.

"That's Tony Hawk," Danny said.

"You know him? You want to watch this?"

Danny nodded.

Ed exhaled and sat on the bed. He watched for a few minutes, glancing now and again at his son's flushed face. "What does Tony Hawk do?"

"He's a skateboarder."

He put his hand back to the boy's head. It still boiled with fever. "Do you want more water?"

He shook his head.

Ed thought of the Emergency Room. Would that be safe? Were the police already after him? He imagined the sleep-deprived doctor doing what he could to stall them, waiting for the local sheriff to arrive.

Ed remembered the fever reducers of Danny's early childhood. "I can go out and get you medicine that would make you feel better. Do want me to?"

"Don't leave me."

"I'm not going to leave you. I wouldn't be long," he assured, though he didn't know how long it might take to find an all-night store in Idaho Falls.

"Don't go. I don't want to be here by myself."

Tears seemed close again. "No. I won't go. We'll get some tomorrow. If you're feeling okay, I won't go." He crawled in bed with his son. "We'll just stay here and watch Tony Hawk."

The program rolled footage of the skateboarder in action. Every trick had a name. Leading with his right foot, Hawk was described as goofy. Goofy or not, he pulled off ollies, nollies, boardslides, bluntslides, lipslides, grabs, grinds, kickflips, pop shove-its, and cab full-revolution jumps. He jumped with precision, purpose, and grace.

Through his fever, Danny made small noises of approval and admiration.

Ed didn't feel like he could pull off anything.

His son eventually fell again into something like sleep. He mumbled, and in his mumblings he asked again for his mother, but the desperation didn't return.

Ed tried to lose himself in the shows that followed. He perked up at the sound of a passing Harley Davidson roaring through the night. Where was the rider going?

His son's smoldering body would not let him sleep. The channel went off the air. Did channels still do that? In Idaho Falls they did.

He was left with nothing except the television's static glow and the darkness everywhere else. And his thoughts.

Thirty-one

Dad lay in the bed next to me, snoring. Our second day in the motel. The day before I had watched television. He went out and came back with medicine, a thermometer, orange juice, and Popsicles, most of which melted in the bathroom sink. "I didn't even think of that," he said. He watched me. He took my temperature a lot.

I'd felt better the day before, but he said we should stay one more day. He said it was the medicine that had me feeling better. "You still have a low-grade fever." He told me we could get back on the road the next day.

I was tired of television. Tired of lying in bed. Dad didn't really talk to me. I asked questions, but he told me just to rest. He seemed sad again, distant. He asked me if it was okay, and then he took long walks.

I imagined Mom at home packing up the house. I wanted to be there for my room. I could picture her in there with garbage bags. I wanted to have some say.

I wanted to see Jimmy, too. Who was he hanging around with while I was gone? Billy Olson? No, too young. Dave Willis? What if he and Dave had become best friends? It's what Dave always wanted. Did Jimmy even care that I was gone? It didn't matter. I'd be gone for good soon enough.

I flipped through the channels, but there weren't many. I found a game show. Dad rolled towards me. His eyes were open.

"How you feeling?"

"Good. I'm fine. We could leave now." He told Mom we'd be home in a week. I would only have one day in Disneyland. Two at the most. Then we'd have to drive all the way back to Michigan. We couldn't do it.

"Just rest," he said, sitting up out of bed. "We want to be sure. Shouldn't mess with a fever. It should be gone tomorrow. Tomorrow we can head out." He pulled his shoes on and started tying them. "Man," he said, "I don't think Bob Barker is ever going to die.

I remember watching *The Price is Right* when I stayed home sick from school." He moved over to the edge of my bed and watched.

"Dad?"

"Hmm?"

"How will we have time to go to Disneyland? We can't go there and get back to Michigan in a week."

His face went blank, but then changed. "I called your mom yesterday while you were sleeping. I told her about you being sick. I told her about Disneyland, too. She knows we're going to be a little longer than a week."

"Did she say anything?"

He told me she said okay. He put his hand on my forehead.

"It'd be great if Jimmy were coming to Disneyland with us," I said.

He nodded. "You feel better," he said. "Could be the medicine, but it feels like you're almost done with this." He looked at me and smiled. Kind of a sad smile. "Mind if I take another walk? I'll bring lunch back. You up for burgers and fries?"

I nodded.

He stopped in the open door. "You know, your mom said too that she misses you. She said she loves you." He stepped out and closed the door, leaving me alone.

The woman on the show missed a new car by one mistake.

Thirty-two

Why did Winters do it? I didn't really care. Where did he take him? That's what I cared about. That's what I was getting paid to care about. Paid once I brought the kid home.

The doctor wasn't too sure of the idea or too excited about my price. But, Kenny only told him the truth when he said it's the best way. The fastest way. The cops will do what they can, but the pressure isn't there. And, the news coverage isn't there—not for any length of time. Not when parents take their own kids. Some parents keep their kids on the road for years, I told the doctor. Sometimes the kids never turn up. They ain't dead. The parent just gets good at staying out of sight. Hell, I almost swiped my own little girl, but I know what it does to the kid. Plus I know how hard it is to get away with. What if someone like me had followed us? Maybe someone even better.

The stewardess came and asked if I wanted a pillow and blanket. On the redeye almost everyone sleeps. My light being on made her anxious, but I waved her off. I wanted to go over what I had.

Kenny told me what he could. We go way back, but he didn't get me this job out of friendship. He cares about that kid. He talked like he was his own.

The mother told me what I really needed to know. She was willing to tell me anything. Winters' mother's maiden name. Likely passwords. Hell, she even knew the guy's credit card number. And, he was still using the same card. After that, it just took a phone call. "Yeah, my name's Ed Winters, and I lost my credit card. I need to know the last ten places it was used." I mean, the person on the other end of the phone's some minimum wage worker just trying to get through a shift. They just read what the screen gives them.

Credit card checks don't always work, not with cons. With Winters it was like goddamn clockwork. From what I could tell, he didn't plan this very well. He used his credit card for almost everything. A ferry across Lake Michigan. Gas in Wisconsin, Minnesota,

North Dakota, Montana. Motels. A fly fishing shop. I didn't get that one. The guy ended up for two days in an Idaho Falls motel. For what I knew, he was still there.

Should have flown into Pocatello, rented a car, and drove up to Idaho Falls. I didn't. I followed a hunch instead. I hopped on a plane to L.A. One-way ticket.

Thing about a hunch is you second-guess it. It was a long flight to L.A.—lots of time for second-guessing.

Winters was in the DNR—knows the woods. He could have been using Idaho Falls as a home base. Stocked up on supplies. Taken the kid into the mountains. He could.

I just didn't figure the guy was at that point yet. He had just called the mother. That phone call made everything real for him. He realized he was a felon—or at least in a helluva lot of trouble. He probably felt alone. Confused. Scared shitless. This guy hadn't planned anything so far—least of all covering up his tracks. Beating it out to the wilderness didn't seem likely. Not yet.

Guy on the run wants someone on his side. Kenny told me about Sheila. Yeah, Winters left her, but that doesn't mean anything's over. Sometimes the ones who get left have the most love to give when the man comes back. They feel like they won something. If you love something, set it free. If it returns, it was meant to be. People believe that crap.

Guy comes knocking on the door, and they go straight to the sack. The pillow talk's all compassion and curiosity. "Tell me where you've been. Are you okay? Of course you were scared. Love's scary. I'm just glad you're here."

People do some stupid shit. Maybe this Sheila would take him in, feed him and the boy, call the mother a bitch and tell Winters that he was doing the right thing. That's what I guessed Winters wanted. Who doesn't want that? On the run? Go some place that feels good. Can't tell you how many guys I've found at an old girlfriend's apartment.

I waved the stewardess back. I reclined my seat and popped off the light. Once in L.A. I planned to watch Sheila's house, watch Winters' credit card. There was a woman in L.A. I walked out on after three months of living together. I planned to look her up.

Maybe she'd moved. Didn't matter. I'd be able to find her. Use her place as a home base. There'd be anger at first, but under it all there'd be bedroom eyes.

She wasn't even all that bad. Good woman, really. And a guy like me could make a helluva lot of money in L.A.—lots of bail skips. I *was* making a helluva lot of money there. Of course, my kid and my ex were in Detroit. You can guess the rest.

Thirty-three

Bleary-eyed and road weary, Ed Winters stood on Sheila's front porch in Pomona. Danny stood behind him on the lowest step. They'd driven non-stop from Idaho Falls. Nearly nine hundred miles. Sixteen hours on the road. Wanting to be sure about the fever, they didn't leave the motel until noon. On the drive, Danny chattered about Disneyland, talked about animals, slept. Other times he stared out the passenger window, zombie-like. It was four in the morning when they came into town. Ed found a parking lot a few blocks from Sheila's. He'd let Danny keep sleeping in his seat. Crawling into the cot, he tried for sleep of his own, but nothing happened. He stared up into the gray darkness of the van, listening to people dragging their feet past on the sidewalk on their way to early morning shifts or on their way home from who knows where. Ed listened. And, he thought.

Seven o'clock. Sheila would be up getting ready for work. At least he guessed she would. He looked back at Danny, smiled, and then turned back towards the doorbell. He'd told his son that the house belonged to an old friend of his. Danny didn't ask for more, and Ed didn't tell him more.

He rang. He stepped back and smoothed his hands over his hair one last time. He swallowed the throbbing pulse in his throat.

"Ed? What are you…" She looked past him to Danny. "What are you doing here?" she asked, her voice more whispered than the first time she'd started the question. She was dressed for work. Business outfit. Makeup. She looked great.

He shrugged. "That's a big question," he said. "You got some time?"

She studied him for a moment. Then she stepped forward and hugged him. "Of course. Let me just call in to work and tell them I'll be late. Come in." She looked at Danny again. "Both of you come in."

Ed released her. Her arms felt good around him, her breasts pressed against his chest. He could have held her for a long time. "If this is no good," he said, "just tell me. I know this might be no good. We don't have to come in."

"No," she said. "It's all right. Just come in. Come in and sit down. You look tired."

He said he was tired. "We're both tired."

"I'm not tired," Danny said, smiling. He looked ready for the biggest roller coaster Disneyland had to offer.

Sheila had toaster waffles for Danny. Coffee for Ed. She fussed around them in the kitchen, more like a waitress than Ed's ex-lover.

"You can sit down," Ed said. "We're fine. Danny's got waffles, toast, juice. He's a kid, not a football team. Just sit down."

She smiled and asked if he didn't want something more than coffee.

He shook his head.

"I'm just going to let Chance in," she said. She opened a door off of the kitchen, whistled, and then pushed the door wider for a bounding golden retriever.

"You have a dog?" Danny nearly shouted.

The dog ran straight to Ed. He rubbed his hands through the dog's muzzle and scratched generously behind its ears. "You still remember ol' Ed, huh boy?"

The dog's tail thumped against the table leg.

"He misses you. He was a wreck after you..." She stopped and looked at Danny. "Do you have a dog, Danny?"

He shook his head. "My mom's allergic."

"You could play with him if you want. There's a small yard back there."

Danny looked at Ed.

"Sure," he said. "Go play."

The boy stuffed nearly half a waffle in his mouth and then poured some milk in around it. "Phanks foa va waffls," he managed to get out. He ran towards the back door.

Ed still held Chance's face in his hands.

"Go on, boy," he said. He pulled his hands back, releasing the dog to his son. "Go play."

The two, boy and dog, burst across the threshold. Laughing, Sheila closed the door after them. "They'll be good for each other," she said.

Ed nodded.

Ed and Sheila walked into the living room, where he settled onto the couch and she onto the recliner. They were quiet for a moment, and then he told her everything.

"You can't do it," she said.

He nodded. "I know. I already figured that out over the past couple of days."

In the backyard Danny shouted for Chance.

"It wouldn't be right," he went on. "What kind of life would that be? No stability. No roots. It wouldn't be fair to Danny. This has all been about me. I realized that in Idaho Falls. But, it can't be about me. It has to be about him."

They sat for a moment in silence. The tinkling of Chance's license and collar came in through the windows.

"What are you going to do?"

He lay back on the couch. "I don't know. I know I'm taking him home. If I could leave the van with you, I'd like to fly him home. I have to call Susan. I have to..." His voice trailed off. "I don't really want to think about it. I'm too tired to think about any of it."

She moved from the recliner and sat on the edge of the couch. She brushed his hair from his forehead and then rested her hand on his cheek. "I understand, you know."

He looked at her.

"I understand why you had to leave. I didn't for a long time. I was really hurt. But then I slowly realized that you had to do it."

He told her he was sorry that he'd hurt her.

"You look so tired," she said.

"I am."

She stood up. "Go into my room," she said. "Go and get some sleep. I'll tell Danny that you're going to sleep. He can play with the dog, watch television. I'll go into work for a few hours and then come home. I'll pick up some steaks."

He sat up and held his head in his hands. "I want to ask you how you've been. I want to know. I'm just so damn tired." He looked up at her. "How have you been?"

She smiled at him. "I've been okay. Just go into the bedroom and get some sleep."

"This probably isn't good. If you're seeing someone … I should just go find a place to park the van. I have a cot in the van."

She said she wasn't seeing anybody.

"Good," he said. "I mean, I wouldn't want to make anything awkward or difficult for you."

She told him to go into the bedroom. "I'll tell Danny," she said. "He'll be fine. I won't be at work long."

At the bedroom door he pulled her to him and hugged her. "I did miss you," he said. "I know I didn't call, but I did miss you. My leaving had nothing to do with you."

"I know. Just go in and get some sleep." She kissed his forehead.

Ed lay in the bed, smelling Sheila on the sheets. He closed his eyes. He needed to call Susan. He needed to call the airport. He needed to be ready for whatever was going to happen. Would Susan and John press charges? What would it mean? Jail? Prison? Would it help that he was bringing Danny back after only four days? They were thoughts that nearly launched him from the bed to the phone, but in time the thoughts blurred into a fitful sleep.

Thirty-four

Saturday. Scrambled eggs slid from Sheila's spatula onto Ed's plate. He thanked her. Last night she had told him the couch was silly. They lay in her bed and found each other in the ways that they knew. Her skin in his hands felt better than anything he'd known in a long time.

"What time is it?" he asked, patting his hair.

"After nine."

"Danny's really sleeping."

She nodded. "Chance hasn't moved from his bed. He didn't even move when I opened the door to let him out. They really gave each other a workout."

"We all got a workout," he said, grinning.

"Ed." She smiled.

They moved into the living room and watched the morning news. Ed dreaded that there might already be something about him and Danny, but there wasn't.

"I'm going to call Susan around noon. I'll tell her we're flying back tomorrow. I'll try to explain. Hell, I don't know. But I know I'm taking Danny to Disneyland today. I know that much. I have to take him."

"We're taking him," Sheila said.

"Okay. Good. We're taking him." He kissed her.

The doorbell rang. They looked at each other. Ed felt something hot and uncomfortable run through him.

"I guess just act casual," he said. "If it's the police, don't try to cover for me. I don't want you getting into any trouble."

Sheila went to the front door. Ed listened.

"Hi, Sheila," a man's voice bellowed. "Is Ed here? I thought I saw his van out front when I drove by."

After the greeting, they talked more quietly. Ed could only pick out a few words from the other man. He heard the word "fire." Why couldn't he place the voice?

"I'll be right back," Sheila said. She came into the living room. "There's a man out here who says he fought fires with you. Joe

Anderson?"

He tried to recall his comrades, but he knew them more by their sooty, sweaty faces than by name. Joe sounded familiar, but Joe always sounds familiar.

"Ed?" the man called. "You decent?"

Ed shrugged. "I don't know, tell him to come in."

The man came into the room. Mustache. Long brown hair. Jeans. Combat boots. Ed couldn't place him. He wore a punched out, thin trench coat, though the weather certainly didn't call for it. His body bulged under the coat. It was thick at the neck. He looked like he could pass for Kenny's body double. His face shined with sweat. "Ed, Christ. You're looking at me like you don't even recognize me. Joe Anderson?" He shrugged his hands into the air.

Ed looked him over again. "It sounds familiar."

"Familiar? Man, what have you been smoking? I'll always remember your face. I felt like I had a brother in you."

Fighting the fire, some of the guys did develop almost a soldierly love for their comrades. It hadn't happened for Ed, but maybe this guy had bonded with him more than he knew.

"Sit down," he said. "Help me remember."

Sheila offered to get him some coffee.

Ed studied the man. Maybe there was something familiar about him. Maybe not.

Joe began to sit, but then popped up again and crossed the room. He opened a closed door. "Hey, this the bathroom… Oops, no." He closed the door slowly. He looked at Ed. "There's a kid in there."

He smiled. "That's my son. That's Danny."

Joe sat in the recliner. "Your son? Man, I thought I knew you. Blazing fire all around us, and you were holding out on me."

Ed shrugged. "Didn't mean to. We're taking him to Disneyland as soon as he wakes up. Which shouldn't be too long." Ed just couldn't place the man, and he hoped he would leave. "I gotta hop in the shower soon. We want to make a full day of it."

Sheila came into the doorway. "You take anything in your coffee, Joe?"

He told her black was fine. She handed him the cup and then

sat on the couch next to Ed.

Joe took a few sips. He looked at Ed and Sheila. "I actually go by Butch," he said.

"Butch?" Ed repeated. He squinted up toward the ceiling. "That doesn't ring a bell, either."

Butch nodded. "It shouldn't."

"Okay," Ed said, sniffing a little laugh.

Butch set his coffee cup on a side table. He inhaled and then spoke. "I want you to both keep sitting like you're sitting. Don't go jumping up. Just listen."

"I don't..."

"Just shut up. I want to tell you how this is going to go down. There are some options here." He moved forward to the edge of the recliner.

Ed and Sheila looked at him, puzzled.

"Your ex is paying me to bring Danny home. I'm going to bring the kid home..."

Something hot flashed through Ed.

"I told you not to start jumping around, goddammit. Just listen. One way or the other, I'm taking the kid back to his mother. You can fight me. That's fine. Your kid comes out of the room and finds me putting your head through a wall. Or, you realize now that it's over. You give up. Nobody's hurt, and your kid doesn't have to see anything ugly."

"You can't just... You can't just come in here like this. You can't..." Sheila stammered.

"I can't? Why? Are you going to call the cops?"

Butch walked across the room and stood, arms crossed, in front of Danny's door. "What's your choice, Ed?"

He sunk deeper into the couch. "I was going to bring him home. I was calling his mother today. You don't have to do this." He ran his fingers through his hair.

"Cut the shit."

"I'm serious. Ask her."

Butch looked at Sheila. "Don't bother. I'm already invested in this. I gave you two options. Take one."

Ed sighed, rubbing a palm across his forehead. "Look, I'm taking him home. Disneyland today and a flight back to Michigan tomorrow. You really don't..."

"Ed. Shut up. What's your choice?"

He shrugged. "I give up. I'm not going to fight. You tell me ... you tell me what we're going to do here to make this easy on Danny."

Butch uncrossed his arms and rubbed his palms on his thighs. He sighed. "It might not be easy. For one, we're not fucking going to Disneyland."

Thirty-five

Ed stood in Sheila's room. He didn't turn on the light, knowing that he didn't really have anything to pack. In the living room Butch asked Danny questions. Listening to them, he could barely move. The bounty hunter's arrival had left him shocked, stunned. They'd told the boy that Butch was an old friend.

He slumped onto the bed. What did this all mean? He'd never see Danny again. Even if he could afford to fly to Paris, a courtesy visit was out of the question. They sure as hell wouldn't send the boy back to the States to spend time with him. Danny would be at least eighteen before Ed would see him again. It was over. They'd have a plane ride together. Loud engines, a small bag of peanuts, and then nothing. At eighteen, would Danny even want to see him again? Would he care?

He could tell them that he realized he'd made a mistake. He could tell them that he was about to bring Danny home. But, they'd probably believe him about as much as Butch had.

The night before he had wondered if Susan and John would press charges. Of course they would, especially after paying Butch at least ... what? Five thousand dollars. Maybe more. They'd press charges.

What about the police? The courts? Would he get less time because he'd only had Danny for a few days? Probably not. Kidnapping was kidnapping. The records would show that he didn't even have visitation rights. That wouldn't be good. Ten years in prison? Could it be that much? What about eight years—one year for each state line that he crossed. Wouldn't even one year in prison be enough? Ed had a friend who worked as a guard at the Marquette prison. He asked him once about the raping. "Does that shit really happen? Is it that bad?" The friend nodded. "It's that bad."

He stood up and walked over to the sliding glass door. Open it. Run like hell. Butch wouldn't come after him. He had Danny. He'd get his money. Why not? Alone, he could live on the run for years. Would the cops even try to look for him once the boy was home? What would it hurt? He worked the lock until it clicked open. He slid the door back slowly.

Danny. Alone with two strangers. Sheila, sure. He knew her, but he wouldn't be with her long. He'd be with Butch. He'd be scared. His father took off out the back door, hopped the fence, ran. The story about Butch being an old friend wouldn't hold together. The kid would be scared. Would Butch have any compassion for his fear? But it was one flight. That night he'd be home with Susan and John. The kid could handle one day. It wouldn't be that bad.

Thirty-six

Dad opened the bedroom door and came out into the living room. Sweaty, he looked at me and smiled. Then he looked at his old friend, Butch.

"Here's how we can do it," he said.

"Do what?" Butch asked.

"Get you back to Michigan to see your old man."

"My old man?"

"Yeah, your old man. Your father. You just told me he's dying of cancer. You just told me you didn't think you'd have the money to get back home to see him." Dad said he could ride with us in the van. "There's plenty of room. We could even split up the driving. Drive by day and by night. Take us three days. Four days tops."

"What are you ... I don't think so."

Dad sat on the couch next to Sheila. "It's the best way," he said. "I'll be paying for gas. I have to make the drive anyway. And, it will give me a little more time with Danny. You're an old friend. You have to let me do this for you."

"Look..."

"I'm asking you. Please let me do this for you. Please. I'll pitch in an extra five hundred on top of whatever they're paying you. Just do it this way."

I didn't understand everything Dad was saying.

He looked at me. "Danny, it would mean no Disneyland. We'd have to get on the road today. But, we'll make the ride fun. We'll stop and I'll buy you one of those hand-held video things. I'll buy you a bunch of games."

"Game Boy? You'll get me a Game Boy? To keep?"

"If that's what it's called, sure. Can't expect you to spend any more time in the van staring out the window."

"Mom won't let me have a Game Boy."

Dad smiled. "I will, though. I still have some say, right? I am your dad. It will be a gift from me. It will help you break up that long flight to Paris."

I still wanted to go to Disneyland, but I'd always wanted a

Game Boy.

"Five hundred?" Butch asked.

Dad looked at him. "We'll stop at an ATM as soon as we get on the road."

Butch clapped his hands and then rubbed them together. "Okay, then. Let's go see the old man."

Dad's friend waited for us on the porch. He left the door open. I hugged Sheila. She was nice. I crouched down and hugged Chance.

Dad put his hand on my shoulder. "You sure you're okay with missing out on Disneyland?"

I nodded. "Your friend has to see his dad. He's dying," I said.

Dad nodded too. He hugged and held Sheila for a long time.

On the porch he thanked Butch again for doing it this way. I didn't really know what was going on.

Thirty-seven

Dad and his old friend didn't say much to each other. Maybe it was hard when someone's dad was dying. They talked about the road, about how many miles we'd gone, about how hard the mountains were on the van. It overheated, and we had to pull over at a rest stop.

Dad didn't say much to me either, even while we sat around waiting for the engine to cool. He looked at me a few times and asked me how I liked the games. I told him I liked them. Then he smiled at me before walking away to look at the peaks. But, really, you could only play games for so long.

We climbed back into the van. Butch got into the driver's seat.

"Seems better now," he said, squinting at the dashboard. "Maybe we'll start on the downward slope pretty soon."

"Maybe," Dad nearly whispered. His voice was sad again.

I picked up my Game Boy, looked through my games, and then put everything on the seat next to me. I looked out the window, but I'd seen enough of the mountains. It all looked the same after a while. I started reading through the brochures we'd picked up in the fly shop.

"Dad!" I shouted. "Dad!"

Butch's eyes flashed into the rearview mirror, studying me. He gave me the creeps.

Dad turned around. "What? What is it?"

I handed him the brochure. "Look! Look! There were grayling in the Madison. There were grayling where we were fishing!"

"What?"

I told him to read it.

"No kidding. There were grayling right where we were fishing."

"Grayling?" Butch said. "Like that town in the middle of Michigan?"

Dad nodded. "It's not just a town. It's a fish, too. It was a fish first."

"A fish?"

"I might have had one on. One of those fish I lost might have been a grayling."

"Maybe," Dad said. He said anything was possible.

"Grayling," I said. "Grayling right where we were fishing. Right there on the Madison. That's so cool."

Dad looked back at me and smiled. "Yup."

"What do you mean it's a fish? I've done some fishing. I've never heard of a grayling."

I explained what it was to Butch. I described it like Dad had described it to me. I described the big fin and everything.

Dad watched me, smiling. "Good," he said. "Good. You didn't forget anything. Just find a way to talk about grayling from time to time, and you'll never forget what you just said."

"Doesn't sound like anything I've ever seen. I've caught some fish on the Au Sable, too. Never saw a grayling," Butch said, maneuvering the car around a guard-railed corner.

I told him it was because they weren't there anymore. "They were over-fished, right Dad?"

"That's right," he said. "That's right. That's how you start to know stuff. You repeat it and you think about it, and you'll never forget."

"I don't think I'll ever forget grayling," I said.

Dad turned around and looked at me. "It's not just grayling," he explained. "It's anything. If you want to remember anything, you have to work. You have to work, right?"

I nodded. I studied the brochure again, wondering if I'd come close to catching a grayling. "Man," I said, "I wish I would have caught one."

Dad nodded. "That would have been something," he said. "But at least we know they're around somewhere in the lower forty-eight, right?"

"We've gotta get one some time," I said.

Dad turned back around and looked out the window.

I watched him for some time. It wasn't long before his jaw changed. It wasn't long before he wasn't smiling anymore.

Thirty~eight

Interstate 80 took it out of them. They tried to push on, but finally took a motel about twenty miles outside of Lincoln, Nebraska. The room flickered with television light. A pizza box lay flopped open on the dresser next to the television. Next to Ed, Danny snored quietly. Butch's frame took up the doorway where he smoked. The cherry of his cigarette glowed, moving from his thigh to his mouth.

Ed shut off the television.

"That was pretty good what you did," Butch said.

"Huh?"

"That stuff back in L.A. The story you cooked up about my dad dying and me needing a ride back to Michigan. Shows that you think on your toes."

"I don't know about that," Ed said.

"You have to think like that in my line of work. You'd probably be good."

"Good?"

"Yeah. A good bounty hunter. Maybe I could train you."

Ed snickered. "I don't think I could get down the intricacies of putting someone's head through a wall."

Butch laughed. "Most of that stuff is just talk. I'm not good because I can fight. I'm good because I can think." He flicked his cigarette, and it exploded into sparks in the parking lot. He closed the door.

Ed said he didn't think he'd be good. "Thinking really isn't my strong suit. Fucking up, now that I can do."

"There are a lot of fuck ups in this business, too," Butch said. "You'd fit right in."

Ed walked over to the pizza. He picked up a piece, but then set it down again. "I mean, I cook up this lie so we can take my van so I can spend more time with Danny. A thousand miles later I've barely said boo to him. Does that sound smart?"

Butch didn't answer.

"So, I'm paying five hundred bucks to watch my kid play games and sleep."

Butch put a few things on the nightstand. They clanked and tinkled. "What did you expect? What did you want to happen?"

"I don't know. More than this, I guess. My kid's heading off to France. I might be heading to jail. I probably won't see him again until he's eighteen—maybe longer. I just hoped we would talk more."

"Time is time. He'll remember this. You don't drive this many miles and forget it."

"Yeah, but what will the memory be? A long, boring drive with his old man?"

"You got the other stuff you told me about. The fishing. He'll remember that."

Ed sat on the end of the bed. "Well, that didn't even work out. No cutthroat. No..." He sighed. "What does it matter, really? What does it matter? He's gone. I had a son, and now I don't have a son."

"You still have a son."

Ed pushed his fingers through his hair. "You know, I didn't even know who the hell I was until I became a father. Nothing ever felt solid or real. Even getting married wasn't any great turning point. Susan and I lived together for three years before we were married. We got married, we went to Mackinaw Island for a weekend, and we came home to the apartment we'd always lived in. Nothing changed. It wasn't until we had Danny that I felt different. It was weird, too, because having Danny meant that I was less important. Not only to Susan, but to myself, too. You know? It was like nothing that I used to care about mattered anymore. But I didn't care. I saw that everything I used to care about was pretty stupid compared to caring about my kid."

"Makes sense," Butch said.

"I left Sheila to be closer to Danny. That was a big loss. But now, there's nothing I can do—no sacrifice I can make to be near him. I might as well be dead. I don't even think it's really sunk in yet. I don't know that it will until he really leaves. I'm afraid of what I'm going to feel like when he's really gone. Sometimes I can barely breathe now. I don't know." He stood up and walked to the pizza again. "Cheese," he said. "I've been eating cheese pizza since Danny was four. Even when I was on my own I kept ordering cheese pizza. I still do. I used to like everything. Now, just cheese."

Butch picked up something from the nightstand—something that dragged and sounded like a chain. "The road wore the hell out of me. I'm going to sleep like a rock."

Ed sighed.

"Did you notice?" Butch asked.

"Notice?"

"Did you notice that I didn't sleep the whole time we were on the road? Even when it was your turn to drive, I stayed up."

"Yeah, I guess."

"Once I hit that mattress, I might as well be dead."

"I don't..."

"I have to put these cuffs on you," Butch interrupted. "You don't take chances in this business. Do you understand?"

"I'm not going anywhere," Ed sighed. Even as he said it, he held out his left arm.

Butch found it and clicked the cold metal around it. "Lie down. I'll just do the other end to the bed frame."

Ed lay with his arm dangling over the bed.

"I'll hang the sheet down over it so the kid won't even notice," Butch said.

Ed closed his eyes and tried to sleep. He listened to Butch undress and get into bed.

"Everything you were talking about," Butch said into the silence that had settled into the room, "about wanting to be dead and everything being over. I don't know. It sounds like giving up to me. I just figure that if you're alive you live. You find something to become, and you live." He rolled over. His snoring soon came, rumbling like the threatening of a coming storm.

Thirty-nine

Coming into Marquette on U.S. 41, they crossed the Chocolay River. Butch was driving. Soon after they came upon the outskirts of Harvey, crossing the Big Creek, Cedar Creek, Cherry Creek and Silver Creek. They passed the A&W, where Ed had taken Susan on their first date. Lake Superior soon spread before them, gray and choppy out to the horizon. An iron ore freighter was moving imperceptibly into port.

"Pretty up here," Butch said. Though he was driving, his vision was drawn constantly from the road to the lake. "It's like an ocean," he said.

Ed did not sense the beauty. If anything, the landscape around them was stark. The ominous lake, the smoke and metal of the power plant and on their left, somewhere hidden behind the trees, was the Marquette branch prison. Ed had never seen it, but always felt its gloomy presence any time he drove by. The empty prison gift shop stood near the highway. Not long ago it was full of leather goods made by the prisoners: wallets, belts, watch bands. Then there was a riot, and prison officials punished the prisoners by closing the gift shop. Surely Ed wouldn't go there. Not to a maxi.

They climbed a rise that would soon spill them down into the small city but, before they did, Butch pulled into the parking lot of an out-of-business Pizza Hut. Ed looked at him.

"I like to keep the exchange spot neutral," he said.

"What? Why are we here?" Danny asked. "We're almost home."

Butch opened his door. "I just need to talk to your dad. Just stay in the van for a minute. We'll have you home real soon."

Ed got out and walked over to one of the windows of the restaurant. There was nothing inside. It had been gutted, stripped of everything. The shape of the outside of the building was the only thing that indicated it had ever been a Pizza Hut.

"Ed."

"We used to bring Danny here when I'd come home from field

work. We'd sit right there," he said, pointing to a corner of the empty building.

"Ed. What I'm getting paid, I'm getting paid to bring Danny home. Not you. You can leave now. Take the van and leave."

Ed looked at him. "Might as well face the music, right? I'll have to some time. Probably be better if they didn't have to track me down."

Butch leaned against the building. He shook his pack. "That's the thing," he said, holding a cigarette in his lips. "Nobody's going to kill themselves tracking you down." He lit the cigarette and took a drag. He exhaled. "But if you stay here. If you just let them have you, and the mother presses charges, the music you face could be pretty harsh."

"Prison?"

"I don't know. Maybe. Maybe not. You'd think not having your son would be punishment enough. Why bring something else on yourself?"

Ed looked at the van, but a glare on the windshield kept him from seeing Danny. "I guess I have to say goodbye."

"I'll give you some time."

Ed nodded.

"What will you do after? I mean, after you say goodbye."

"I guess I'll take the van."

"Where?"

"I have a little place not far from here. In Gwinn. I guess I wouldn't go back there. There might be someone snooping around."

Butch shrugged. "I doubt it, but I guess staying away makes sense."

"Yeah, I won't go back there right away."

Butch lit another cigarette. "So, where will you go?"

Ed looked up. Then he looked at the ground. "I don't know. I have a friend who's a deck boss on a trawler up in Alaska. Maybe I'll head up there."

Butch snickered smoke out his nose.

"What?"

"I don't know. What is it with you outlaws and Alaska? Gotta go to the ends of the earth. What do you think you'll find? I can tell you. Cold. Helluva a lot colder than anything you've known."

"Find? I'm not look… It just seems like a safe choice."

"Safe?"

"The police."

Butch dropped his cigarette and crushed it under his boot. "They're not going to be looking for you. Even when you had the kid they were barely looking for you. Kid's home now. Case closed. Why would they spend any energy on you?"

Ed shrugged.

"Don't you have any idea where you should be headed? Not a clue? Why the hell would you choose Alaska?"

"I don't know. I got a friend up there. Maybe I want to catch a grayling and write to Danny about it," Ed said defensively. "Maybe I want to take a fly rod and do it. Maybe there'd be something to that—something worth a letter."

"You don't need a reason to write. You just do it. And, from what the kid's brochure said, you don't need to go to Alaska to catch a grayling. Hell, there's probably grayling in California."

"What? What's that supposed to mean?"

Butch pulled out another cigarette. "I'm done here," he said. "You gotta figure this out yourself, I think. I can't… Just, you know, I got a phone call to make. Just go say goodbye to your kid. I can give you ten minutes."

Ed started towards the van.

"I'll tell them, too," Butch called to him. "I'll tell them how easily you gave up the kid, and how you were taking him to Disneyland. I'll tell them that it seemed like you were probably going to bring him home anyway."

Forty

Dad crouched down next to me in the parking lot. His eyes were red. I started to cry.

"What? Why are you crying? Don't cry, Danny."

"It's just everything," I said. "I'm sorry I'm crying. I just can't..." I fell onto his shoulder, sobbing.

He cried, too. Then he talked. "I'm going to try to stay in your life. I will stay in your life. I'll write. You'll have to write me first, but then I'll write. Will you write?"

I nodded.

He pressed a piece of paper into my hand. "This is Sheila's address. Don't write to me in Gwinn. Send your letters to Sheila's. She'll know how to get them to me."

"Where are you going to be?"

"I don't really know, yet. I'll know soon. Sheila will know. Just send the letters to Sheila's."

I sobbed again. "I don't want to go, Dad. I don't want to go. I hate this. It's all Mom's fault."

Dad put his hands on my shoulders and pushed me back so he could see into my eyes. "It's not your mother's fault. She didn't do anything wrong. You can't believe that."

"But you said she fell out of love."

"If she did, she didn't do it on her own. I don't think I was easy to stay in love with. I don't know, maybe it's not anybody's fault. Or, it's mine. But, it's not your mother's. And, it's not John's. You have to be at least friends with him. You like him, right?"

I nodded.

"Good. You should. It's okay to like him."

I fell on him again in tears. "I still don't want to go. I don't want to leave anything."

He held me for a long time. I felt him crying, too.

I loosened my grip, and Dad stood. He looked over by the Pizza Hut, where Butch was standing by the door, smoking a cigarette. Butch pointed to his wrist.

"Butch is going to call your mom. She's going to pick you up here."

"Why?" My crying let up. I was confused.

"I just need to take the van and go. There's something I have to do, and it can't wait. Your mom will be here in a few minutes."

I cried again and tried to hug him.

"I have to go, Danny. I can't."

He pushed his fingers through my hair. "I know everything is changing and seems really scary. I know what you're feeling. But, look at Montana. You and I didn't know anything about it, and we went there. We found a river and we fished. You can make things that you don't know or understand work. Sometimes you have to."

"We didn't catch any cutthroat."

"I don't really think that matters. Do you think it matters?"

"I guess not."

He hugged my head into his belly. "Just remember to write me. I want to hear how great you're doing over there. I know you'll be doing great."

"Okay."

He told me to go over and stand with Butch. "He's a friend," he said. "You'll be fine. Your mom will be here soon."

He climbed into the van, and I couldn't see him anymore. He pulled out on the highway and disappeared.

I walked over to Butch. I was still crying.

"I'm calling your mom right now."

"I don't understand," I said. "Why did he have to go away?"

Butch started punching numbers into his cell phone. He looked out at the highway. "He's asking himself the same question right now," he said.

Forty-one

The Mackinac Bridge stretched shore to shore in the dim distance. It was hazy. It cut in and out of view as U.S. 2 snaked around Lake Michigan's northern beaches. Five miles of steel and concrete suspended between St. Ignace and Mackinaw City. Some people said it was impossible. But there it was.

Christ, five guys died while building the damn thing. Still, they didn't quit.

Where was Winters? Where the hell did he go? I had my money. I shouldn't have cared, but I did. I couldn't shake him from my thoughts even after three hours of driving.

It was dusk by the time I hit St. Ignace. It'd been over two months, but I called my ex.

"Butch? What do you want?"

"I want to take Tara to the zoo on Saturday."

"Can't. She'll be at soccer camp. You have to give a little more notice. You can't just…"

"Okay. Okay. I'll call ahead next time."

"Why do you sound like that? Where are you calling from?"

"Just windy up here. I'm calling from St. Ignace. Up near the bridge?"

"I know where St. Ignace is. Why are you there? Wait, don't even tell me."

"Hey, it's the nature of the work."

"I've heard that before."

I snickered weakly. "Yeah." Turning, I put the wind to my back. "So, when will I see her next?"

"When you see her, I guess. Summer weekends fill up fast."

"Well, tell her I called."

I found the campground Winters talked about. The Mighty Mac arched solidly over the choppy, chaotic straits. I decided I'd sleep in the rental car. Wouldn't be the first time. Helluva lot cheaper than motels. Saving money is pretty damn close to making it.

Middle of the week, I almost had the place to myself. Only one other camper. Some guy by himself in a pop-up. I watched him stabbing a long stick into his small fire. It took a while to get myself moving, but I started collecting some sticks of my own.

Branches leaned against each other. Twisted paper stuck in the spaces. You never forget how to build a fire. My old man showed me.

I hoped the best for Winters. At least that he would make some good choices—some choices that would mean something. He could make some really bad ones. This would be the time a guy could really fuck up.

He'd headed west on U.S. 41 when he pulled out. Was he going to Montana? That would be something at least. He could stop at a sporting goods place along the way—pick up a fly rod. Grayling on a fly rod. That'd be something to write the kid about. Could even send a picture. Can't easily forget that. "My old man is something else," the kid might think in some Paris café. Might eventually get curious enough to hop on a plane back to the States. It wasn't impossible.

At a rest stop somewhere in Minnesota, Winters still could have some sun left—no matter how dark it was getting in St. Ignace. Lots of stretches of grass at rest stops. Good place to practice casting. I'd seen fly fishing on television. He'd need to practice.

Where would he go after the river? Of course. South. L.A. Right? Why not. He already knew the highways he'd have to take. Good woman with a dog. That was his chance at something.

Hell, dumb ass was probably headed for Alaska. Get himself washed overboard on Bristol Bay, freeze to death. Or, end up a cokehead in Dutch Harbor. Some of those little towns have the ugliness of a city. Sure have the drugs.

Freedom? A clean slate? Don't know what guys expect to find on those damn boats. More men are wrecked by them than saved. I was up there twice. Lots of guys on the run up there.

Winters. Poor bastard.

Fathers cut off from their kids in some way. How many were out there? I looked at the silhouette of the other camper alone by his fire. Christ, there must be thousands of us.

I'd call again the next day. Vickie would be at work. Maybe I'd get Tara on the other end. She'd be excited to hear from me. I'd set up a time to meet her. Maybe the mall. Whatever she wanted. It was always easier to pull off when Vickie wasn't in the middle of it.

The wind off the lake grew colder. The bridge glowed above the blackness. I felt a little better. I struck a match in the darkness—a small prayer candle for Winters. I touched it to the kindling.

Forty-two

Ed Winters kicked a path down the snow-covered driveway. The snow was on everything. The yard. The trees. The roof.

He reached into the mailbox and grabbed the bundle of letters. He shivered. The weatherman had predicted the cold snap.

Walking back towards the porch, he flipped through the letters. As it had before, the strange international postage jumped out at him. France. Another letter from Danny. Ed wanted to feel excited. He couldn't. He'd had other letters from him, and something about them always felt forced. The weather. What he was studying in school. Watching familiar movies in French. They never felt like letters from a son to a father. They felt more like the letters Ed was required to write in high school when the school officials had decided that it would be a great experience for all of the juniors to have pen pals in Portugal. It wasn't a great experience. It was a monthly burden. The burden could be felt, too, in the strained letters that the Portuguese students wrote in return. There was only so much one could say to a stranger living in another country.

When Ed would write back to Danny, he tried to be as particular as he could. He wrote about the things they'd done together, especially in the last two weeks they'd been in each other's company.

Ed opened the letter. It was meager. A paragraph.

Dear Dad,

How are you? I really hope you're doing good. You'll never guess what I did. Well, I caught a grayling. Yup! Did you know that grayling are native to Europe? I went fishing on the upper reaches of the Dordogne River. It was full of grayling. I caught a bunch! Their back fins are big just like you said. Dorsal fin, right? You'd really like them. Remember all that fishing we did in Montana? It made me good. I can really cast good, now! John said that when you come for a visit, he can show us how to get back to that same spot. You and I can go fishing and finally catch some

117

grayling together. I promise we will catch some. When do you think you can come here? I'm leaving this letter on the kitchen table. John said he'll mail it for me tomorrow.

I love you,

Danny

P.S. John, here. Say Ed, I just wanted to tell you that I recorded some great footage of Danny catching those fish. I'll make you a copy and send it very soon. You'll be proud of him. Quite the fisherman.

Ed read the letter three more times. In that time, more snow began falling from the sky and swirling around him. He smiled at some of the words. Native to. Upper reaches. Dorsal fin.

The kid always did love new words.

"Being from Michigan, you didn't think we ever got snow in California, did you? Probably a little depressing."

Ed looked up at Sheila standing on the porch in her bathrobe. She held two steaming cups of coffee. Seeing Ed, Chance broke from her side and ran playfully through the yard. Blades of grass poked up through the tracks he left in the snow.

"This?" Ed said, swinging his arm out toward the rare snowfall all around them. "This is nothing. All of it will be melted by this afternoon. It's already melting."

Chance galloped all around him.

Ed moved towards Sheila, wanting to show her the promise in the paragraph he was holding.

Haunted

Feeling along the wall, Rachel hoped for no new marks on her son. The hallway was muggy with summer. She stopped in his doorway. Franky sat in the spotlight of his reading lamp holding up the bottom of his shirt with his left hand and smoothing the palm of his right over his chest. He looked up. "This one's bigger," he said. The rest of the room hung dark around him.

She stepped from the doorway into the center of his room. "What woke you up? Did you feel something? Was it a dream?" Dreams at one time sent him scurrying down into bed with Frank and her.

"I just woke up," he said. "It doesn't hurt. They don't hurt."

She sat on the edge of his bed and pushed her fingers through his damp hair. The pear-shaped red mark was an inch or so under his right nipple. "It looks like a rug burn," Rachel said. "What are you doing in here at night? Do you think you're sleepwalking— walking into things and then getting back into bed?"

He shrugged.

"You called out to me. Do you remember calling out?"

Franky flipped his pillow over and lay his head on it. "I remember," he said. "I was awake. I just wanted you to see it."

"We're going to have to tie you into this bed."

He smiled.

She pulled the sheet up to his neck. "At least it doesn't hurt."

He shook his head. "It doesn't," he said.

She asked if he could go back to sleep, and he said he thought he could. She wasn't sure what time it was. She stood.

Franky's skinny arm reached up and the lamp snapped off, leaving Rachel uneasy in the sudden darkness. She slid a foot toward the doorway, waiting for her eyes to begin to adjust. She told

Franky to have a good sleep.

"Grandma thinks it's Dad."

Rachel stopped, inhaling deeply through her nose. "That what is Dad?"

"The marks. That Dad comes into my room and leaves them. She saw it on a show about ghosts. She said they could be love marks."

She turned towards the bed's shadowy outline. She couldn't see Franky. "She said that? She talked to you about something like that?"

Franky didn't answer.

Shaking her head, Rachel sucked her lower lip between her teeth. "Not like I even—but why ... why would your dad do something like that to you?"

"Grandma thinks that he doesn't want to be forgotten."

"Forgotten?"

"She just thinks that he wants us to remember that he was a part of this."

Rachel sighed. "It's not a ghost. You're doing something in your sleep. It's not Dad." She stepped toward the door. "Your grandma shouldn't have said that."

Rachel went back down the hallway to her own bedroom. Lisa shifted around in the sheets.

"What's up?" she asked sleepily.

Rachel got into bed and rolled her back to her. "Nothing. It was just a dream again."

Lisa shifted closer and put her arm over her. Her breasts flattened against Rachel's back.

"You're usually up later than me," Rachel said. "Do you ever hear him in his room moving around?" She felt Lisa prop herself up on an elbow.

She moved her fingers in Rachel's hair. She said she never heard him moving around. "Why?" She lay down and put her arm over Rachel again. She kissed the back of her head.

Lisa's arm felt heavy and warm and Rachel wanted it off. "I have to get up early tomorrow. Four o'clock."

"I'm not—"

"It's too hot to sleep like this. I don't want to be held."

Lisa lifted her arm away and rolled her own back to Rachel. "Are you going to talk to Kawaski?"

Rachel exhaled. "No. It's nobody else's business."

That morning she'd found a note in her box. It read,

What you're doing is perverted.
Frank is turning in his grave.

"Somebody always makes it their business," Lisa said.

"Would you just be quiet about it, please?"

"Fine."

Rachel said nothing else. When she heard Lisa sleeping, she wanted her arm around her again. "I'm sorry," she whispered.

She left for the post office at four thirty, where she worked as a sorter. Lisa was a carrier. Nobody at work knew that they'd been lovers for eight months—or at least nobody let on up until the note. Since Frank's death two years ago, her co-workers didn't say a great deal to her and those that did asked her how she was getting by without him. Some asked her to go out at night to the bar with them, but she never did. "Frank wouldn't want you to be alone," they said. She'd heard some of the other carriers refer to Lisa as a dyke.

Her mother-in-law's pink Mary Kay Cadillac was in the driveway when Rachel arrived home at three. She wished she could afford a sitter. She wished her own parents were still alive. She didn't like owing her mother-in-law anything, but she needed the help with Franky—especially in the summer.

Judith was in the kitchen washing dishes. Her off-white blouse segued perfectly into her beige skirt. Her makeup was flawless. She looked forty-five, though she was nearing sixty.

Rachel sat at the table in the breakfast nook, an addition Frank put on the house three years ago. It was an anniversary present. Ten years together. "I meant it when I said that you don't have to clean while you're here," she said.

Judith looked at her and smiled. "I don't mind."

"Where's Franky?"

"Next door."

Rachel looked out the window into the Johnson's backyard. It was lush with flowers. Franky and David were throwing a football with David's dad. Mr. Johnson threw perfect spirals. Did the Johnsons know about Lisa?

"I spoke with Father Stricket on Sunday."

Rachel cleared her throat. "About what?"

"About you and what you're doing—the way you're living your life now."

Rachel stood. "Judith, you had no right—"

"He said he's seen this before. He says it can happen when someone has a great loss. He said it especially happens with widows." She explained that Father Stricket said that the pain can be so great that the wife rejects who she was and by rejecting who she was she can reject the pain.

Rachel sat down again. "You had no right. This isn't—"

"I'm just trying to understand," Judith said. "I don't have anyone to talk to about this. I can talk to him." She poured a cup of coffee.

"This isn't anybody's business. I don't want other people to know." She wanted Judith to leave. "I don't know why *you* would have to talk to someone."

Judith pulled out a chair and sat at the table with her. "Because I don't understand this. It hurts me what you're doing. He was my son. Franky is my grandson."

Rachel set her face in her hands.

"I lost Joe to an early heart attack," Judith said. "Then Frank went the same way. It's hard for me to think that his entire marriage was a lie. All I have left is Franky." Judith sipped from her coffee.

Rachel spoke into her palms. "It wasn't a lie. It wasn't like that. It's just that after … it's just I realized, I came to see—" She stood. "None of this is about you. Why do you even make it your business? Why do you care what I do?"

Judith took another sip. "I worry about Franky."

"Well, you shouldn't."

"Has he told you about the marks?"

"Yes," Rachel said, her voice rising. "Yes, he did. And, he told me what you said about them. That was a terrible thing to say to an eleven-year-old boy."

"Maybe it *could* be Frank. He was certainly the kind of man that made his feelings known. Maybe it isn't, but a little boy—"

"I know what kind of man my husband was."

Judith walked her coffee to the sink and poured the rest down the drain. "Father Stricket said that you're confusing Franky by having that woman here. He says—"

"Please don't call her *that woman*. You don't know anything about her. This isn't your business. Just let it go." Rachel walked out of the kitchen in tears.

When she was nearly asleep, the phone rang. She picked up.

"I didn't see you today," Lisa said.

"I know."

"Were you *trying* not to see me?"

"No," Rachel lied. "Sometimes, though, I think maybe we shouldn't talk so much at work."

"Oh?"

Rachel switched the phone to her other ear. "Just why make things hard, right?"

"Sure."

"Lisa—"

"Look, I was just calling because we had talked about me coming over tonight. Do you even want me to?"

"I want you to. Come over. I want to see you."

"You could act more like it."

"I'm sorry. I am. Just come over later." Rachel unplugged the phone from the wall and closed her eyes.

That night, Franky's moaning ripped her out of sleep. She stumbled down the dark hallway and into his dark room. "Turn on the light, Franky."

He whimpered something about his legs.

She found her way to the bed and then found the switch for the reading lamp. She closed her eyes against the sudden light. "What's wrong with your legs?" she asked, squinting at his body twisted up in the sheets.

"I don't know. They're sore."

She pulled his pajama bottoms down. "Oh, Jesus." His thighs were blemished with red marks. "What did you do? Do you think you might have done this? I think you're sleepwalking."

Franky looked at his legs and started to sob. "Is Daddy mad at me?"

Rachel pulled him to her chest. His tears soaked warm through her pajama top. "He's not, honey. Your dad isn't doing anything. Grandma should never have said that." She told him that they'd figure out what was happening. With the darkness pressed all around them, though, she wasn't sure if they would.

"I think you're sleepwalking. You're getting out of your bed and bumping into things is all." She held him until his sobbing idled down into sleep. Lisa was still sleeping when Rachel came back to bed.

In the morning, Rachel found another note folded in her box.

Dyke.

Something nauseating tingled under her skin. She threw the note away. She went to one of the stalls in the ladies' room. Everything came to her. The note. Franky's legs. She wept against the toilet.

Just before the trucks left at eight, Lisa found Rachel in the break room. They were alone.

"I only have a minute," Lisa said. "I'm glad I got a chance to see you."

Rachel swallowed. "I don't think you should come over tonight."

Lisa paled. "Why?"

"It doesn't have to be every night. I should spend some time with Franky."

"We do spend time with Franky."

"I think maybe just I should sometimes. Maybe you shouldn't be over so much."

Lisa stared. "I have to go," she said. "I have to get my truck out."

Rachel had trouble concentrating on her work the rest of the day. When not thinking about how she might have just lost Lisa, or Franky's legs, she studied her co-workers, wondering who would have left the notes. They seemed to look at her differently—like maybe they'd written the notes together.

Arriving home, she walked through the front door and heard Judith get up from the kitchen table and go out the garage door. A moment later, her car started. Rachel went to the picture window. The pink beast backed down the driveway, turned into the street, and then pulled away. Judith didn't look back at the house.

A note in Judith's handwriting told Rachel that Franky was playing at David's house. Under the note was a pamphlet titled "God Still Loves You". Rachel opened it and read.

Homosexuality.

Concerning this issue, the Bible is absolutely clear. Homosexuals do not go to heaven. There is hope for homosexuals, however. Christ can convert homosexuals and lesbians and make them true children of His. The truth is that people who are homosexual are that way, not because of genes, but because of sin. The potential to be homosexual is in every person. We are born as sinners, and have potential to do any kind of sin, including homosexuality.

Rachel closed the pamphlet and crumpled it in her fist. She threw it against the refrigerator.

Lying in her bed, she couldn't nap. She couldn't understand what was happening to Franky. Could there be something in the house? Could it be Frank? Even with the sun coming through the blinds, she shivered.

She closed her eyes. "Frank," she whispered, "are you doing this? Are you angry with me?"

She said she didn't understand why he would hurt Franky. "Is it because of Lisa?" She paused. "I love her, Frank. This is not something I'm doing to hurt you. It's not an experiment. If it makes any difference, I love her for the same reasons I loved you." She opened her eyes and looked around the room, half expecting to see a shadowy outline of him sitting on the bed. She closed her eyes again.

"She takes care of me, like you did. She wired more outlets into the kitchen, like you were going to do."

She told Frank that it doesn't make their marriage a lie. "I don't think I was unhappy in our marriage. Maybe you were. I know I didn't give to you, in this bed, like you wanted me to. But, I didn't cheat on you. I wasn't seeing other women while I was with you. Your dying ... it just pushed me into what I guess I always should have been. We got married so young."

She said that Lisa was good with Franky. "She loves him. You should see them together. She's really helped him with his reading." Rachel cleared her throat. "Remember when we talked about if either one of us ever died young that we wanted the other to find love again? That's all I did, Frank." Exhausted, she closed her eyes and listened to the settling sounds of the house in the walls. She decided she'd call Lisa after her nap.

When she woke, the blackness was solid around her. The alarm clock read five thirty in the morning. Her panic subsided when she realized it was Saturday—her day off. Padding down the hallway, she stopped by Franky's room. He slept peacefully. She went downstairs and made coffee. She sat in the backyard and watched the sun rise. She felt foolish, but still wondered if her talk with Frank had made a difference.

At eight o'clock, her telephone rang.

"Did you read the pamphlet I left for you?" Judith asked.

Rachel didn't say anything.

"I'm only trying to help you."

"Judith ... I don't ... I think I'm going to have to find a different sitter."

"Rachel—"

"I'm serious. I don't think it's good for me to have you in my life all the time. I just don't—"

"You should know then that I talked to a lawyer."

Rachel went still. She could hear her ears ringing.

"I really think that Franky should live with me for a while. You're not making a good home for him right now."

"Judith—"

"You'd still be able to see him. The lawyer thinks I have a small chance. I took pictures of Franky's legs yesterday. The lawyer said I'd have to be willing to talk about everything. I told him I would."

Rachel felt a numbness creep through her. "You know I have nothing to do with those marks," she whispered.

"If it goes to court, Rachel, you'd have to explain them. You'd have to talk about that woman."

Rachel sniffed, and tears welled in her eyes. "Why are you doing this?"

"I'm not doing anything, yet. I just wanted to let you know that I talked to a lawyer. I'm going to give you more time."

"More time. I don't even—"

"You just need more time to think about all of this. You should talk to someone—maybe a psychiatrist."

Rachel sobbed.

"I don't think we should talk about this anymore right now. You're not in a good place. I'm going to let you go. I'm going to let you think about it," she said, as though ending a Mary Kay sales call with an ambivalent customer.

Rachel's coffee went cold. She imagined scenes from the courtroom. How would she explain Franky's bruises? Would they believe sleepwalking? How would she explain Lisa? Would any of it be enough that they would find her an unfit mother? She sat numbly.

Franky shuffled into the doorway of the kitchen in only his briefs, his hair matted in places, sticking up in others.

Rachel grinned at his skinny little body. His legs already looked better. "No pajamas last night?"

He said it was too hot.

"But you slept through the night? No dreams … or anything?"

He nodded, and a wave of relief rushed through her.

"Hey, sorry I was sleeping and didn't make you dinner. What did you eat?"

"I called Grandma and asked her how to make hotdogs in the microwave."

Rachel imagined how that might play out in court. She shook her head. "You should have gotten me up. I would have gotten up."

He shrugged and walked over to the cereal cupboard.

She watched him. She could barely breathe when she saw the scratches on his back. It looked like something fingernails would have done.

As calmly as she could, Rachel planted the idea into Franky's head that since it was Saturday he could sleep at the Johnson's house if David invited him to. Usually she didn't like to have him away from her on the weekends and said no to his requests for sleepovers so, hearing her suggestion, he dashed from his half-finished bowl of cereal. Rachel heard the sliding glass door close a few minutes later. Alone in the house, she shivered. A half an hour later, Mrs. Johnson called to ask if it was okay for Franky to sleep over. Rachel said it was okay, but then asked to speak to Franky.

"You can sleep over there tonight," she said. "But, you have to wear pajamas."

He said he would.

Rachel was surprised by what she found in the yellow pages. She made a few phone calls and talked to a couple of different people. One was fairly certain that he could help her. She told him almost everything over the phone. He said he would come by in the evening. She spent most of the day in the backyard thinking about everything. Losing Franky to Judith. Franky's cuts. The trouble at work. Lisa. She didn't call from her truck at lunch like she normally did. Why wouldn't she be angry, hurt?

The doorbell rang at seven.

The man she opened the door to wore white: white shoes, white socks, white pants, white shirt, white vest, white blazer, and white tie. He was overweight, but kept his hair neat and parted to the side. He smelled of oranges. She invited him in.

"I'm really hoping that this won't be a waste of your—"

He closed his eyes and tilted his face toward the ceiling. "Oh, there's activity here. I'm tingling."

"Really?"

"It's upstairs. I can feel it and I'm not even up there." He told her that they should sit down for a minute so he could explain what he did. "I'm not a ghost buster. I hated that silly movie," he said, taking a sip from his tea. He'd brought his own bag and had asked only for hot water. "That movie only confused people." He said he didn't have fancy equipment. "I talk to the spirits," he said. "I reason with them. And, when necessary, I wrestle with them—trying to drive them away. They are often easily dislodged, their footing in this world being so tenuous, anyway."

She nodded. "I don't have a lot of money."

"If I'm successful, we can work out a payment plan. Seeing as I was granted this gift, I have to be flexible."

He went upstairs. Rachel sat at the kitchen table and listened. For a time, there was nothing except his footsteps creaking in the joists. Then, she could hear him talking. He paced around to the different bedrooms. He stomped. He shouted. Rachel never would have guessed that he'd have been capable of such volume. She tried to sip coffee, but could only wince at his outbursts. Her heart felt like a caged wild bird.

Nearly an hour had gone by when he came downstairs. His hair was wet, and his face was drawn and pale. He'd sweated through his shirt, vest, and jacket. He shook his head.

"What?" She felt instantly alone.

"You've got something ... something up there bigger than me. It wants to stay."

"Frank?"

"No, it's not your husband. This ... whatever it is. It's ancient. Its hold in this world is strong." He asked for a glass of water. He fell into a seat at the kitchen table.

"But then what do I do?" she asked after he finished a second glass.

He shrugged. "I'm not sure. You don't have to worry about paying me, though."

"Is there ... do you know anybody else?"

He grinned apologetically. "I'm considered one of the best in the state." He scratched his nose. "Though most won't attempt exorcisms anymore, I guess you could try a priest."

"I'll move. I'll just move."

He nodded. "Some people do. Though, spirits aren't always connected to a place. Sometimes they're connected to a person."

The windows were dark. She hadn't turned many lights on around the house. This man would soon leave. She could feel herself shaking.

"I did talk to your husband briefly. He's almost gone—almost moved on." He said Frank spoke mainly gibberish. "He kept saying something about good outlets."

Something hummed in Rachel's spine. "How could you have—"

He stood, but had to steady himself on the back of a chair. "I'll call you if I think of anything. I'm sorry."

When his taillights disappeared, she felt watched. Hunted. She was no longer alone in the house. She picked up the phone and dialed.

"I need you to come over."

"I'm not sure I want to," Lisa said. "I just think—"

"I need you to. I'm afraid." Rachel wept. "I'm sorry about everything."

"Don't cry like that. I'll come over there. Don't cry, honey. I'll come."

"I'm so afraid."

"I'll come over."

Rachel sucked in a breath. Though she'd just heard herself say it, she wasn't really afraid. Fear was a part of what she felt, but it seemed far below the surface of her anger. She felt cornered. She wanted out. "I'm going to talk to Kawaski on Monday about those notes. I'm going to file a harassment—"

"Okay, Rachel. Okay. We'll talk about it when I get there. I'm leaving now."

Rachel sucked in deep breaths to calm herself. Everything about her life was out of her control. She held the phone until a woman's voice told her that if she wanted to make another call she should hang up and try again. If she needed help, she should dial the operator. The woman repeated her message again and again. "Oh, fuck you," Rachel said to the phone. The woman's voice, authoritative and patronizing, soon became a grating alarm. Rachel thought of Judith and punched in her number.

Judith picked up.

"Call your lawyer."

"Rachel? I don't—"

"Call your damn lawyer if that's what you're going to do. Call him. But, if it goes to court, and I win ... you'll never see him again. I just think you should think about that."

"Why are you—"

Sick with adrenaline, Rachel slammed down the phone. She sucked in long breaths through her mouth.

Waiting for Lisa's headlights to wash over the front window, she went to the landing. She looked up. She wanted to see it—see something. Each step grew gradually darker until the last few disappeared into the blackness at the top. Something like mercury rose up her spine. This was her house.

She ran up the stairs and stood in the dark hallway. Whatever was there had never touched her, but something was there with her. She could feel its hate. Her eyes wouldn't adjust to the darkness. Something cold swept over her, through her.

"What?" she screamed, trembling with more anger and fear than she had ever known. "What do you want? Why are you here, you bastard? Why the hell can't you just leave us alone?"

NUFOINFO

The daughter sits across from me gnawing on a fatty ball of meat stuck to the end of a fork. She's engrossed like a dog at a raw-hide.

I should have made up an excuse to leave the moment I saw her.

My chair is turned sharply, keeping the daughter as much as I can just a blur in my side vision. I concentrate on the heavyset mother who sits smoking at the end of the vinyl-covered table. Her name is Sara Chib. She's wearing a hooded sweatshirt with a large picture of Tweety Bird on the front.

Sara is why I'm here. She is my witness.

I already know that my two-hour drive was wasted. There's nothing here worth writing down.

The choked interior of the place is black around us with only one fluorescent rectangle of light burning overhead. It feels like the only light on the entire Abbaye Peninsula. We are fifteen miles north of L'Anse in Upper Michigan on Aura Road. I could barely find the place, even with my GPS. The female voice said, "You have arrived," but the shotgun shack itself was another three miles down the road. That should have been my clue to turn around and go home.

I didn't, though.

I guess I still feel a little excitement at the possibility of every investigation. There's something in the night sky more than just us. Every one of those stars ... each is a sun. Many hold planets in their gravitational pull. It's naïve to think that ours is the only planet with life. Gathering these stories—this evidence—has always made me feel like I'm actually a part of something significant.

After a half hour of fruitless backtracking and double-checking, I flagged down a snowmobiler for directions. When I said the last name, he looked at me like I was asking directions to the nearest chemical spill. Then, he pointed.

From outside comes the steady rhythm of the husband shoveling. I saw him when I came in. Well, I saw his eyes. Every other part of his six-foot frame was covered. Ski mask. Big military parka with fur around the hood. Choppers on his hands, and moon boots (appropriately enough) on his feet. He glanced at me when I pulled in and then bent back to his work of hoisting snow off the driveway.

A steady snow has been falling since four o'clock, leaving inch after lazy inch, accumulating imperceptibly but irrevocably, so that the Abbaye Peninsula residents will find themselves in the morning as I often feel ... buried.

"Don't now!" Sara says, turning to her daughter.

I look across the table. The daughter has the entire piece of meat in her mouth, stretching one of her cheeks out like a bullfrog's throat. Sara reaches over and eases the fork out again. The hunk shimmers with saliva.

The daughter looks sheepish, like a scolded lapdog.

"You won't get it at all if you keep that up," Sara says. She turns back to me and reaches for her cigarettes. She sighs.

I write her name on the Sighting Report.

"NUFOINFO. What's that stand for, again?" She's watching me write.

"The National Unidentified Flying Object Information Network for Openness."

She reaches for her pack of menthols. The menthol is the only thing that keeps me from asking to have one. I burned up my last cigarette just outside of L'Anse.

"Now that name's a mouthful," she says, lighting up. "You give it that name?"

I explain that I'm just a field investigator. It's a worldwide operation. On top of hundreds of field investigators, there are corporate trustees, functional directors, regional directors, state directors, foreign directors. Hell, NUFOINFO even has a dive team! If something does come into our atmosphere, it has a better chance of hitting water than anything else. I've given some thought to training for the dive team, myself. With the Great Lakes so close, I'd have the chance of getting called in on something pretty big.

"They pay you?" she asks.

I shake my head again. "No. I teach at the university." I don't tell her that it's been seven years and I haven't made tenure. They're not sure what they're going to do with me next fall. My department chair is holding his cards close to his chest on that one. At his suggestion, I knocked out an article on the underrated importance of understanding non-verbal communication in a marriage. It's under consideration at a few journals. I doubt it stands much of a chance at publication, but if it does get published, it could buy me another year.

"What you teach?"

"Psychology."

She takes a long drag and then exhales toward the light. "I don't like that Dr. Phil. Comes across like he's got all the answers, but I don't think he knows how things really work. He talks down to people and tries to make their problems seem so easy to solve."

I smile in agreement.

Sara motions toward her daughter. "She likes him, though. Likes bald guys. That's why she's acting pretty good around you. Her grandpa—my dad—was bald. He died a couple years ago."

Sara looks as though she could cry. It's not what I want to happen.

I drag my hand over my smooth scalp. "Grass doesn't grow on a busy street," I say, laughing.

Pulled from her melancholy, she smiles. "That makes sense. My husband's got hair like a wolf man."

The shoveling suddenly stops. Aware of an absence, I look across the table. The daughter has stopped, too. Her eyes search the windows.

"Shh. Shh," Sara says.

The shoveling resumes a moment later.

Sara looks at the door. "He's starting at the top of the driveway again. Way the snow is falling, he might be shoveling until sunup. He's gotta be able to get that truck out in the morning."

It reminds me that if I don't move this along, I could be spending the night here.

I start by asking her the basics. Date of the event. Time of the event. Duration of the event.

"I'm really only doing this because I feel like I have to," she says. "It feels like it's my duty."

I nod. "Well, let's get to the shape of the object." I have a whole list to read to her. Blimp. Boomerang. Cigar. Cone. Circle. Cross. Diamond. Disc. Egg. Fireball. Flash. Oval. Sphere. Rectangle. Square. Star. Teardrop. Triangle.

She thinks for a moment. "Never stayed one thing altogether, really. It looked like a diamond when I spotted it over what I guessed was Sand Bay. It seemed to be moving closer. As it did, it turned into a flat line, then a teacup, and then an upside down V. When it was at its closest, it was kite shaped and stayed that shape longer than any of the others."

I take a moment and set up the mini-tape recorder. Sara shakes a cigarette from her pack and lights it with the cigarette that she is just finishing.

I hit record. "Tell me everything," I say.

"Well, I was out on the—"

My cell phone starts vibrating in my pocket. Pulling it out, I check the screen. The area code is 701. That would be my ex-wife calling from North Dakota.

I inhale deeply through my nose and turn the tape recorder off. "I'm sorry," I say, "but I have to take this." The one bar of connection is barely flickering. "I'm going to step out on your porch."

I answer. "Hold on, Julia," I say. She starts to talk, but I hold the phone to my chest. I pick up the cigarettes. "Do you mind?"

Sara, smiling, shakes her head. "Nope, go ahead."

I light up and take a minty drag. It tastes terrible, but the nicotine is there. "I won't be long."

It's cold outside. And dark. Nothing really exists—just charcoal silhouettes in the faint lightness that the snow reflects to this place. The snow is still falling steadily, but seems to be lightening. Patches of starry sky come through the clouds. That's what the weatherman had predicted. His forecast had shown a green mass, then a clearing, and then another green mass coming in from the west.

The husband is halfway down the driveway. What he has finished shoveling for the second time is already layering with snow again.

I haven't spoken to Julia in over a year. It's been six years since the divorce.

I take another drag, flick the lozenge-flavored cigarette into the snow, and lift the phone from my chest to my ear.

"I have, at tops, five minutes, Julia."

"Hi, Gale."

"I'm in the middle of taking down a sighting."

She's quiet for a moment. "I figured as much," she says.

"It's a good one," I say. "Lots of classic stuff, here. Shifting shape to the craft. Kite-shaped when it gets clo—"

"Isaac's on his way to see you. He's on a bus."

My son. I've seen him twice since the divorce.

"Gale?"

My neurotransmitters have my heart going wild. "Why?" I manage to ask.

She swallows. "I don't know."

I didn't fight for custody ... just handed Isaac over to her entirely. I wrote alimony checks like I did any other monthly bill. The divorce knocked the wind out of me. Around that time, the guy who did field investigations for the eastern half of the U.P. quit. I stepped up and took both halves. I lost myself in it. It was a way to stay sane.

She's quiet for a moment. "Dan and I split up," she says.

I get that little flicker you get when you hear another person's bad news. It makes you guilty, but there's always a part of you that quietly revels in it. "I'm sorry, Julia."

"I just wanted you to know about Isaac ... just wanted..." She takes a quick breath and then exhales. "He's vulnerable right now. I just want you to give him as much of yourself as you can."

I start to pace the porch, trying to walk off the cold that's crept through my coat. "You know I'm not very good at that—you said so yourself."

"Well, you have to try."

"Julia … I mean … why? Why does he even want to see me? How did he decide that—"

"I don't know, Gale. He's pretty lost right now. He's grasping at straws."

"Doesn't he remember me? Doesn't he remember that I was never—"

"He doesn't talk about what he remembers. All I know is that he wants to spend some time with you."

I squeeze my forehead with my free hand.

"Gale … after Dan and I … I just don't think Isaac is in a good place."

"Why did you let him leave? I'm not going to be able to help. You should have—"

"Just try."

I take in a deep, cold breath. "I don't think I can." I hang up the phone and then shut it off. I shiver in the cold that's penetrated everything. Everything is still except for the falling snow and the father's Sisyphus-like struggle with its accumulation.

Going inside, I lower myself into my chair and sit at the table again.

Sara exhales. "You look like *you* saw a U.F.O. Wasn't bad news on the phone, was it?"

I shake my head. "Let's just finish up." I take a few deep breaths, trying to counter my adrenaline.

Sara doesn't speak right away. "You want to turn that on," she says, pointing at the tape recorder.

I nod and push the button. I don't bother picking up the pen. Without asking, I take another of her cigarettes. She does the same.

She says something about the U.F.O. being off-white in color and that it seemed bigger than a plane. She goes on about two lights in the center being bigger than the other lights. "The smaller lights looked like running lights or something, but not the normal red and blue/green lights you find on a plane. They were twinkling white and blue and looked different from any lights I'd ever seen on something in the air."

She reaches over and pets her daughter's hair. The daughter

seems calmed by having so much of her mother's speaking in the room. Her fork and meat sit on a saucer on the table in front of her.

"My dad was in the air force," Sara says, "so I've been around planes more than the average person. This was no helicopter nor tilt wing craft that I can imagine."

She says that after a few minutes of hovering, the craft flashed away higher and out of sight. "Zoom." She shakes her head. "Nothing man-made coulda flown like that."

"What's her name?" I ask.

Sara looks at me and sees that I'm looking across the table at her daughter. She smiles. "This is Barbara."

I nod.

We sit for a moment, and nothing else moves in the room except for Sara's hand, the tiny sprockets of the tape recorder noiselessly taping our silence, and the smoke rising from our smoldering cigarettes.

The rhythm of the shoveling comes to us again. Barbara stirs and reaches for her fork. She gnaws the meat gutturally.

Sara reaches out and shuts off the tape recorder. "You have everything you need from me?"

I've been so unprofessional. I drag the tape recorder to me and begin to shuffle the report papers together. "I think that should be everything."

Sara rises, goes over to the sink, and begins to scrape chicken bones from dinner plates into a small garbage pail. She looks out the window into the blackness in the direction of the shoveling sounds. She works slowly, absently.

When I saw Isaac last, he was fifteen years old. I'd flown into Bismarck for a psychology conference that my department head had highly recommended for professional development. Julia and Isaac made the two-hour drive down to see me. We went to lunch. I listened while he told story after story of camping trips and fishing trips with Dan. He didn't really make eye contact with me as he talked, but I could feel that he was telling me that he didn't really need me in his life, anyway. He had Dan ... that was clear.

I was relieved when they finally got on the road to drive back home. They didn't end up staying in a motel like Julia had planned. I flew home from the conference two days early. I wasn't in the mood to go to breakout sessions and listen to people deliver boring papers on the behavior of fruit flies or the complex nature of transference.

Packed up, I zip my briefcase shut. Sara is at the sink still, staring out the window. She says something I can't hear.

"What?" I ask.

Barbara is looking across the table as though she is expecting something of me.

Still looking outside, Sara repeats herself. "I said, 'His father was a mean man'."

"Your husband's?" I know the answer, but the question is all I can manage.

Sara turns around. She stares at the floor. "This isn't an easy place to live if you have a lot of anger." She rubs her right hand up and down her left arm. "Sometimes he can't control it."

I feel like I did in the earlier years of recording sightings. The stories always left me stunned by the descriptions of things that couldn't be fully understood.

Sara looks up at me. "I'm sorry," she says, "I just needed to tell somebody."

I slide my hand slowly on the table and watch it move back and forth. "He hits you?"

She steps up and, with both hands, begins smoothing her daughter's hair. Barbara leans into her mother's left palm, closes her eyes, and hums pleasurably. "Sometimes." She looks down at her daughter. "He never lays a finger on her." She sniffs.

After a moment, I stand. "You shouldn't have to live like that. Why do you stay?"

She sits at the table again and reaches for her pack. "I ain't fit to work. Barbara needs me." She flicks up a flame and studies it. "Plus, I love him." She touches the flame to her cigarette. "Let's not talk about it anymore. I hope the other—the U.F.O. stuff—is helpful for you."

I assure her that it is and then fall into my script. "On behalf of NUFOINFO, I want to thank you for contacting us. Every story helps."

"That's what I figured." She brushes at her eyes. "That's why I called."

Outside, I stand in the cold on the porch.

The husband, like a haunting, is just a silhouette moving rhythmically in the darkness across the driveway. Watching him, I know I have "fight or flight" chemicals surging through me. If I say anything, it might just make things worse for Sara.

I need to get past him. I step down the stairs and start toward my car.

He says something to me as I go by.

I turn. "I'm sorry, I didn't hear you."

Pulling off his chopper, he adjusts the mouth hole on his ski mask. "I said, 'so is she crazy?' That's all I need is two of them."

Something burns along my spine and I step closer to him. "Her? Her mind is fine. She's fine."

He shrugs. "U.F.Os? That's a little out there."

Words hover up out of me unexpectedly. "You really need to deal with the source of your anger," I say. "That's the only way."

"What?"

I swallow my heart back into place. "Anger is like a disease. It's contagious. You're a carrier. I know your father wasn't a good man, but hitting Sara ... that's not going to help. You need—"

I'm on the ground. It feels like somebody's trying to pull the gums on the left side of my face free of my teeth. In my side vision, he crouches next to me. I wince when his hand goes up again.

He pulls off his ski mask and wrings it between his hands. "Are you okay?"

His face is framed by wild hair and a thick beard. He stares at me wide-eyed.

"I've never been punched before," I say, dazed. "You punched me, right?" My jaw hurts when I talk, but I don't think it's broken.

He sniffs. "I'm sorry. I didn't mean... Jesus, I'm sorry."

I try to prop myself up on my elbows, but then, light-headed, lie back in the snow.

He's kneeling before me. "Look, don't call the cops. We don't need the cops out here. If I could take it back..."

I roll the hurt side of my face into the snow. It stings more than soothes. I turn back toward him. "You need help," I say.

He bows his head. He whispers. "I know. I know I do."

I watch him for a moment, looking as though he's lost in prayer. "There are people you can talk to," I say. "I know people in Marquette. If you want to change, you can change." The calm and logic of my words surprise me. It's like I'm listening to someone else.

He takes a deep breath, and after it he seems somewhat assembled again. "I'm going to go for a walk. I need to take a walk." He stands feverishly. "You want help getting up?"

I shake my head. "I think I need to lie here for a minute." I pat the ground until I find my briefcase. I pull it up onto my chest and start feeling out the beginning of the zipper.

He bends over, finds his chopper, and pulls it back over his hand. "I just need to move. I need to walk." He lingers over me. "You going to call the cops? Am I going to jail tonight?"

I find one of my cards in the briefcase and hold it out toward him. It's a black rectangle in the night. "Take this. If I don't get a call from you on Monday, I *will* call the police. I'm sure I'll have a pretty good-sized bruise to show them."

He takes the card from me, nods at it, and then starts off at a loping jog down the driveway toward the road. The sound of his footsteps in the snow fades and then is gone.

His dad still has him on the run.

Above me, the rest of the clouds fade slowly away. The pain in my cheek recedes into a dull pulsing. The sky is a black dome spectacle of stars. I stare up into it. My mind's going a mile a minute. After a moment, I can almost see the two brilliant lights on the front and the small orange lights along the side. I can almost hear it, and the idea of it has me feeling astonished. It's a huge presence out there moving towards me. It slides through the darkness ... my son's bus. I don't give any thought to the possibility of life on other planets or what may or may not be in the night sky. My only thoughts are of Isaac out there somewhere rocking sleepily on his seat—unidentified as yet as to what he signifies for me—wanting only to be witnessed and to be heard.

Breakdown

Thousands of insects swarm around the radiant light above the pumps. She stands near the gas station doors. She waits for people to come out. A few women go in the station past her. They glance at her. They will come out, but she won't talk to them. She needs a man. She is sure that a man will come and fix everything. It might take some time, but she will eventually be in her bed, trying to forget the burden of the next day. The next week. The next month.

How much easier it would have been for her not to go. All the way to Flint for a funeral. She hadn't been to one since her husband's. Before that she'd only been to her son's. An anxious boy, his enlisting never made sense. One hundred and forty-eight soldiers died in the 1991 Gulf War. Her Jacky was one of them.

Several lights had flashed across her dashboard as she drove home from Flint. Then the car started to jerk. Something hot flashed up her spine. The car had had enough left in it to get her to the gas station.

A teenage girl nearly hits her with the station door on her way out.

Nobody at the funeral seemed to see her either. Still, when she looked at her dead uncle's face, she remembered his kindness. He had surprised her when he came to the small gathering they had just before Jacky shipped out. He put his arm around her skinny soldier son. "Your future is in boxes, Jacky. People don't think about 'em much, but they need 'em. When you get back, you have a job. You come down to Flint and, hell, I'll make you a shipping clerk." Sitting up late in her dark living room, thinking of her son over in some land she could barely imagine, she would tell herself that he would soon come home to his new job. He had a job waiting, and he would come home to it. The war was going well, and few Americans were dying. Jacky would come home and work in Uncle Walter's cardboard box factory. It made sense—sense enough that sometimes she could climb the stairs back to her bed and fall into something close to sleep.

The door opens again. A man she didn't see go in comes out, moving quickly.

It takes her a moment to speak. "Sir?"

He keeps walking.

"Excuse me, sir? Sir?"

He stops, turns. Wearing a fishing vest resembling her dead husband's, he looks surprised to find that she is talking to him. Small colors freckle the white, fuzzy patch just above his heart. She remembers her husband's word for them. Flies. They look nothing like the houseflies the word brings to her mind.

He looks at her expectantly, smiling. He has big hands.

"I'm sorry to ... it's that my car. My husband's car. Over there." She points. "Something's wrong. It stopped running out on the highway."

He looks towards the car and then around the parking lot and then back to her. "Just died?"

She nods.

He rubs his fingers on his cheek, making a sandpaper sound on his stubble. His lips buckle into an apologetic grin, and his shoulders shrug. "I really don't know anything about cars." He looks around again.

He seems in a hurry, and she almost releases him. Then she doesn't. "Could you just try to look at it?"

The highway drones in the nearby darkness.

He doesn't move for a moment, and then a slight bouncing of his head turns into a nod. "Okay, I'll take a look. I can't promise anything. I really don't know anything about cars."

Walking towards the car, she feels relieved to sense him behind her. He will fix the car. He will know.

"It was my husband's car," she says, when they are both standing in front of it.

"Caddy," he says.

She nods. He knows the make of the car. She smiles.

"Pop the hood."

She goes to the driver's door and opens it. She doesn't know how to pop a hood, but she is relieved to have someone telling her what to do. Her husband did it for so many years. He reminded her that she needed to eat, demanded it. He made her get the pills so she could sleep. He told her to stop the therapy sessions because they only made her worse. He was a man who knew how to keep going, even when things fell apart.

The man comes to her window. "It's a lever," he says. His finger points towards her feet. "It's down under the dashboard. You'll feel it."

She gropes in the darkness.

"I can get it," he says. He reaches in, his hand brushing her nyloned leg. She hears something give, a metallic thunk. "Got it," he says. He goes back to the front of the car and disappears under the opening hood.

She waits, certain that he will find the problem. She hears her own breathing.

He comes back to her window. "Do you have some kind of light? A flashlight or something?"

She thinks for a moment. "My husband's toolbox is in the trunk. There could be a flashlight in there."

He looks at her and smiles. He pats her hand with his big hand. "Okay," he says. "I'll need the keys."

She hands him the keys, knowing that it won't be long before she'll be back on the road.

She'd heard it many times before—the sound of tools jostling against each other in her husband's toolbox. Replacing rotted boards in the porch, fixing the leak in the washing machine, changing out the condenser on the refrigerator. He could do anything. The only thing he couldn't fix was his high cholesterol—even with the pills the doctor prescribed. The heart attack, not a complete surprise, still knocked out the little wind she had in her. With him gone, she couldn't fix anything. Finding the strength to finally change the burned-out light bulbs around her house, she came home with a box of a dozen. They turned out to be the wrong size.

She let the rooms in her life slowly go black. All but one. She moved lamps into the room where she kept all of her pictures of Jacky.

"Found it," the man says, waggling the flashlight side to side. Giving her the keys again, he moves back to the front of the car.

The light flashes around over the engine. She watches it through the space under the open hood. He is going to find the problem. It will be right in front of him. "Got it," he will say. She opens her door, gets out, and comes around to the front so he can tell her when he finds it. She will watch his big hands fix it.

Keeping the light on the engine, he rises up from his stooped position. "Nothing jumping out at me. Like I said, I'm not really good with cars. Does it have a history of problems?"

She looks at him and shivers. "It was my husband's car. He took care of it."

He nods. "Well, nothing's jumping out at me."

They both stare at the illuminated engine. This time last year she watched her television programs—one after another until finally falling asleep in her chair. Her husband counted his pennies, nickels and dimes into sleeves to bring back to the bank. If it wasn't living, at least it wasn't suffering.

A car pulls up.

"What are you doing?" the driver asks. He leaves the car running, its muffler grumbling. He sucks at his cigarette.

Another man. Maybe he can fix it. She starts to say something, to tell him her story, but the man holding the flashlight jumps in.

"Nothing. She just asked me to take a look at her car. It died out on the highway."

The man in the car looks at the woman. Then he looks at the man with the flashlight. He takes a drag. "You don't know anything about cars," he says, talking smoke out of his mouth.

"I know."

The man in the car looks at her again, studies her.

She doesn't like the way he seems angry, reproachful of her. His face looks distorted, but then she sees that it's a thick, black beard. "It was my husband's car," she says. She tells him what happened on the highway. Beyond the new man's car, the lights above the pumps glow fiercely. Beyond them, thick blackness looms over the hum of the highway.

"Sounds like a timing belt," he says.

"A belt?" She thinks of her husband and the vacuum cleaner. "You can replace it?"

He shakes his head. "Not in a parking lot, you can't." He asks her where she needs to go, and she tells him.

"Gladwin? That's not far. I'm sure they've got a phone inside."

"How far is Gladwin?" the man with the flashlight asks. He seems to be asking something else, too. He is stooped under the hood again, waving the light around.

"Not far," the man in the car answers. "Nowhere near where we're headed, but not far. Take twenty minutes or so for someone to come pick her up. Maybe less." He looks at the woman again. "I'm sure they've got a phone inside."

Who can she call? She doesn't know anyone anymore. Since Jacky's death, she knew her husband, and him only because he hadn't left her to her grief. She shivers. "It's cold," she says.

"Yeah," the man with the flashlight says. "These June nights aren't always warm."

"Warm enough," the man in the car says.

The flashlight flickers. He hits it with his hand, and it glows steadily again, but dimmer. "Batteries are dying. Been awhile since you changed them?"

She shrugs. "It was my husband's."

He nods.

"We should get on the road," the man in the car says. He flicks his cigarette and it hisses out in a puddle. He directs his voice at her. "You need to go inside. I know they've got a phone in there. They all have phones."

"I can't imagine who I'd call." Her voice quavers.

The man with the flashlight turns it off. He walks over to the other car and leans down.

She can't hear him, but the words in the hissed whisper of the driver drift to her in pieces. He says something about not having time. Something about this one night to hit the hex hatch. Something about his wife. "They've got a phone inside," he says. "She can call her people."

What people? Who can she call? She doesn't have any phone numbers memorized.

The driver says something about stay if you want to stay, but he is going.

"I don't know what I'll do," she says. "My husband took care of everything."

The men look at her. "You got to go inside," the driver says. "They've got a phone inside. We can't do anything for the car. We can't fix it. They've got a phone inside they'll let you use."

They are quiet for a few seconds.

"We have to get on the road," the man in the car says, shrugging his hands in the air above the steering wheel.

The other man walks over to her and puts the flashlight in her hand. He apologizes. "I wish I could fix it." He jerks his thumb towards the gas station. "You'll have to go inside," he says. "Call someone."

"I don't know who I can call."

"You'll have to think of someone," he says. "There must be someone." He puts his hands in his pockets and looks back at his friend in the car. "We have to go," he says. "We've really only got this one night."

He jogs around to the passenger side of the car. The driver looks at her while the other man gets in. "You'll be fine," he says, setting a cigarette between his lips. "Go inside. You gotta go inside. You'll be fine."

They pull away. Briefly, under the bright light, she sees them talking. The man on the passenger side runs a hand through his hair. A small flame leaps up in front of the driver's cigarette. Then the car becomes a silhouette. Only the brake lights show clearly. They pull out, cross the overpass, and disappear.

She stands before the open hood. It gapes with blackness. She rubs the tips of her thumbs over her fingertips. The cold gets her shivering, but she shakes from something else, too. If she let it, it would shake her apart.

She goes back to the entrance of the gas station. People stop at the pumps, fill their tanks, and leave. Many don't even go inside.

Those that do often come out again as though they intend to take the door off its hinges. Their faces are far away, hurried, looking like they need to be other places. They smack packs of cigarettes against their palms or sip cautiously at the lids of coffee cups. They slow down for nothing.

She doesn't have it in her to try to stop any of them. She stares at the frantic insects deflecting off the lights above.

In her car, she sits for a long time. Dozens of other drivers pull in, gas up, leave. Some of the drivers are teenage boys, like her Jacky had been. A day after she received the news of his death, a sergeant called her. He was with Jacky the night before he died.

"Your son was a night owl. Never saw him sleep much. Good man for guard duty, but you can't keep a man on duty all night." She told the sergeant he'd been the same way at home—not much of a sleeper. "We talked that night—the night before he... He told me about you and your husband and how he missed the both of you. And, he told me he was afraid, too."

She imagines her son pacing in the Iraqi night. What had woken him to leave him alone with the vast darkness of the desert? He had lived with the knowledge that any day could be his last. That was no way for such a young boy to live. Such a nervous boy, really.

"I told him I planned to bring all my men home alive. I really wish I could have. But I wanted you to know that even if he was afraid, he didn't show it. He was as brave as anything. He didn't die because he was afraid. I just wanted you to know too that his last thoughts were of you and your husband."

She thanked the sergeant for the call.

Collapsing onto the steering wheel, she cries for her son. She had cried over him before, many times, but tonight she cries for his loneliness. Her tears are for his tender helplessness. Her tears are for herself, too. The small sobs shake her.

Leaving the car, she starts for the road. She doesn't know when she will get to her house. Fifteen miles. Is she walking five miles an hour? Then she has three hours to go. Or, is she going three miles an hour? Two miles an hour? She stops doing the math. She hopes that someone will stop.

Off in the distance, across fields, the small windows of houses glow, so far away they might as well be stars. Cars pass her, sometimes startlingly from behind, and sometimes from in front, washing her in the harsh brilliance of headlight. She waits for somebody to slow down, turn around.

Trudging over the gravel, she advances from pool to pool of streetlight. Her nylons do little to keep the cold off of her legs, and her feet start to ache in her pumps. She stumbles. The darkness feels thick around her and, ahead, the rows of telephone pole lights will eventually end. She curses her life.

When the street lights are gone, she turns on the flashlight and follows its dim pool of luminescence. Cars continue to pass her, lighting her up briefly, illuminating her black blouse, her black skirt. When there are no cars, she hears the insects in the fields around her. She remembers her husband talking about the hatch— a time when nymphs that had lived in the river for years come to the surface and hatch into their adult form.

She shivers, but can't shiver away the cold. She thinks of the fishermen and their damned hatch. Their damned fish. She wonders if they are cold—standing in the current, casting their lines blindly into the darkness. They won't get out—not for anything.

She keeps walking. She thinks of her son again—alone as he had been in a hostile country.

Writing on the Wall

Walt was always reading something. Standing with the current of the Au Sable's South Branch moving around his thighs, he read the river. The stretch ahead was wide and flat and without riffles. The small, lazy rises near the edges were probably just creek chubs. Fifty yards later, the river narrowed at a bend, and the surface began to flash white with its roughening before it turned out of sight. Just beyond the bend there was a tree down in the water on the left bank and beyond the scum line of the tree a nice hole. He'd finessed a thirteen-inch brookie out of the hole the year before. Thinking of the fish, he pulled his heavy feet from the mucky bottom where they'd settled.

He carried a cloth glove to handle each fish, having read that it was less likely to strip away its protective mucous. Dipping the glove through the surface, he'd hold the fish while gently removing the hook with his forceps. He pinched his barbs flat, so his hooks slipped out easily. Balancing his catch lightly between his thumb and fingers, he'd set it just below the surface in a calm part of the river. He'd stand stooped until the fish would find its bearings and swim out of his palm. It's what he'd done with the brookie the year before. It's what he'd do with any fish. He didn't come to the river to keep fish. He came to forget, even if only for just a few hours.

For others, the river had become a battleground. He couldn't help but read about it. It was in all the fly fishing magazines. Some company in Traverse City owned the mineral rights to the land around the river. They wanted to drill for natural gas and other resources. Fly fishing organizations were fighting it. They called the area sacred and wrote lengthy arguments and raised money. They won the first court battle, but as recently as six months ago it looked likely that the ruling might be overturned in the company's favor. Walt started ignoring articles that dealt with the controversy. After all, the company owned the mineral rights. It struck him as a no-brainer. Fighting. Politics. It wasn't what he wanted on his mind when he came to the river.

He rubbed his eyes, took a long breath, and then started downstream. The sun was close to moving below the trees in the west. The day was cooling. Walt cast to some likely spots and felt the way the rituals of fishing filled his consciousness. Rises. Cover. Hatches. Riffles. They were simple thoughts, but they held off everything else.

He'd only moved a short distance when he noticed another fisherman at the bend below. A footpath ran along the river, and fishermen could pop in anywhere. Walt forced his disappointment down. The new man had as much right to the water as he did. The stranger might be bringing his own heaviness to the river, his own need to forget.

After a moment, the new man wristed his first cast. Walt's disappointment welled up again and soon became anger. He hooked his fly into the hook keeper, wound up his slack, and marched toward the man. Walt had read about such men in the fly fishing magazines. This was the first time he'd seen one.

The new man turned, and his face blanched. Looking Walt over for a few seconds, he tried to smile. He touched his palm to his chest. "Man, scared me," he said. "Thought you were maybe DNR."

Walt looked at the open-faced spinning reel on the other man's pole. He then turned his stare up into the man's face. "What kind of *fly* do you have on?"

The other man turned his hand and looked at his reel. A Mepps spinner dangled and dripped at the end of his line. He looked at Walt and started to grin sheepishly.

"This is flies only," Walt said, pointing at the river.

The other man was bigger than Walt, thicker. Some of the color came back into his face. He stiffened his jaw. "So," he returned.

Walt stepped over to the bank and laid his rod in the grass. He came back to the man. Both of his hands were free, and he knotted them into fists and kept them steady at his sides. "So," he repeated back to the man. "So, I'll take you apart right here."

The river moved around the legs of the men. A wind pushed through the higher branches of the trees. It stirred nothing at their level.

"You're serious," the man said. He blinked. "You're serious?"

Walt didn't release his fists. "This is flies only."

The other man couldn't keep any kind of eye contact. Paling again, he released his line and groped for his spinner. His voice was an octave higher when he spoke. "I mean, I just wanted to take a fish home. No big deal." He set one of the treble hooks into the biggest eye on his pole and gave the reel a few turns. The tip of the pole bent. "It's just that I don't live far from here. It's easy to get to after work."

"It's not right. It's illegal."

"All right," the other man said, holding up an apologetic palm. He started toward the bank, beyond which was the footpath. "Well, good luck fishing," he said awkwardly.

Walt retrieved his rod and watched the other man flash here and there through the woods until he was gone. His heart writhed in his ribs like a dying fish in a creel.

He was a different man from what he'd ever been. Just the week before, in the middle of a sales call, he looked across the desk at the young man who was studying a contract that Walt had given him. "Can't really afford a television ad," the young man said, "but this seems reasonable." He owned a new bookstore, and he was wearing a t-shirt with the name of the store on it. It had been open for a month and a half, and he'd already had t-shirts printed up. Walt had talked him into a month's worth of radio spots. Probably could have talked him into a year's worth. "You know," Walt confessed, "our listeners aren't really book people. We've surveyed them, and they don't read." The young man set his pen down. His smile faded. "Then I shouldn't do this?" Walt shook his head. "You shouldn't."

He had a meeting coming up with the radio station's manager and guessed that they would be talking about his miserable sales numbers. Walt's son had been dead for over a year and a half. His dying was losing some of its strength as an excuse.

Walt had read somewhere that few marriages survive the death of a child. Knowing that what he and his wife had gone through was typical didn't bring him any comfort. He was alone. She was gone, living in a spare room in the basement of her parents' place. Sometimes he'd talk to her on the phone. There was so little of her left that he'd sob after hanging up. He'd lost them both. He stood in the river going numb, the water pushing against his legs as though they were two rotted trunks ready to fall.

Downstream, just past a long stretch of riffled water, a trout rose in the crook of one of the river's elbows. It was a slow, confident rise in the kind of bend where a big trout might linger, waiting for the fast water to wash in feed. The surface where the fish had risen turned in a slow eddy. Perfect.

The fish came up three more times before Walt was able to get within casting distance. They were so consistent, he could almost time the rises. He studied the surface. There didn't seem to be a hatch going on. He stayed with his blue-winged olive—a trustworthy fly for almost any Michigan river. Casting upstream of the hole, he let the fly drift naturally across the surface of it.

Nothing.

Not wanting to spook the fish, he waited until the fly and his line had drifted well past the hole before he tried another cast. The first cast might have been too far from the bank. Hadn't the fish been feeding closer to the partially submerged rock? Walt wasn't sure. He cast again. And again. "What the hell do you want me to do," he said ten minutes later, "put steak sauce on the damn thing?"

He tried two other flies before abandoning the hole. The fish had been seemingly going after anything. And then a blue-winged olive, a mosquito, and a royal coachman drifted right over it within a twenty-minute span. Why wouldn't it come up? How did it know? Leaving the hole, Walt felt a tickling of anger. He suppressed it. The frustrated questions he was posing about the nature of fish were gentle compared to others he could ask about the nature of life.

He'd fished for two hours already and hadn't seen a cabin. The Mason Tract—nothing but wilderness and river. He had read about

George Mason and the donation of property the auto executive had made to the state of Michigan. Fourteen miles of river and the adjacent land given over for public use.

Walt looked around. The river. The trees. The sky above. All of it was darkening toward night. He remembered a book, an old book—maybe even the Bible—which he'd been made to read as a teenager. There was something in it about going to the woods to live deliberately. Something too about quiet desperation. His own desperation felt anything but quiet. It pleased him when his mind put together the sentence, "I went to the woods to live forgetfully." He'd always liked putting words together and had once used the skill to write radio spots.

Living forgetfully. It was a bliss, a reprieve. The water swirling around his thighs might well have been the Lethe River, given the merciful amnesia it cast over him.

In the current at times like this he sometimes felt something around him—something bigger than the trees and the river. Something bigger than him, something he had never been able to name with any confidence, and yet a presence. It was the something that for the longest time he'd blamed for his son's death. It was the something, too, that he thanked on nights like this for making water move.

Walt tied on a new leader and a new fly—a pattern of his own making. He used a size 8 hook, black thread and dubbing for a body, dun hackle, and finally deer tail to make a large, white parachute wing. He squeezed fly dressing between his thumb and forefinger and pinched it over the hackle. The fly glinted with the floatant. For a short time it would be easier for Walt to see without the glare of the setting sun on the surface. Then it would get dark. It was coming into the time when he often caught a better-sized fish. He worked the stretches along the bank.

Something glowed orange on his left. A man was sitting on a log smoking a cigar. He was gray-haired and had a fly rod and wicker creel. Walt smiled when the older man nodded. The other man's waders were shiny with water. Smoke drifted up.

"Just getting in?" Walt asked above the talking of the river.

The other man brought the cigar to his mouth, took a puff, and shook his head. "Been here since noon. Just getting done."

"Can't find your car?" Walt asked, smiling.

The other man grinned, and the tip of his cigar flared in front of his face. He exhaled languorously. "Just not ready to go home yet."

Walt nodded, knowing the feeling. He waved a mosquito from his face. "Fishing good?"

"Fishing's always good."

"Yeah," Walt said.

He fished on and soon had trouble seeing. Fishing at night took from him one of his favorite aspects of fly fishing. He liked to watch his fly. He liked to see it when a fish rose and pulled it under. It was a part of the everything that made fishing good for him. With the darkness fading in around him, he became aware of the dark thoughts crowding into his mind. He didn't want them. The steps to the Fisherman's Chapel were just around the next bend. He would get out of the water there.

There was no moon. Walt caught his breath after climbing the flight of stairs. The inside of the chapel was like a cave. What he'd read only a few days before was haunting him again. The article had been in one of the magazines in the radio station's lobby. He had tried to abandon the words when he could see where they were going. It was no use. He couldn't stop reading. It related that by nine years old children understand death and can anticipate their own. They can live their last hour in the terrifying fear of knowing that it will be their last hour.

Standing in the blackness of the chapel, he imagined his son, his little Tommy, treading water in the bottom of the well. It was Walt's idea to move the family to the country. He had wanted the old property and had even found the ancient well charming ... as charming as the skeletal remains of the old Nash rusting to nothing-ness in the woods behind the property. He and his wife had warned Tommy about the well so many times. How could it have been that after two days of searching that's where they'd found his water-logged body? How many times had the boy called up the shaft of the well, and heard as a reply only the echo of his voice coming off the wooden curbing? Treading in the cold, Tommy knew he was going to die.

Walt dropped to his knees and cried into his palms. He lived in the sobbing like he had lived in the fishing. It consumed everything.

In time, he held out a hand and steadied his shaking body against a wooden beam. His fingers found something. Someone had carved something deep into the wood. He traced his fingers along what turned out to be letters and spelled out the word *faith*. Searching above the word, he touched along more jack-knifed braille and found the other word. *Have.*

Have faith. How many times had he read it in sympathy cards or heard it as consolation from family and friends? Have faith. In what? In the cruelty of life? In its ephemeral nature? Have faith that in the end our lot is suffering and that everything we build up and come to cherish will be slowly or quickly taken from us? He fought these black thoughts. Tonight, having found the words, he wanted them to mean something. He recalled the peace he'd felt on the river, the cleansing. Staying on his knees for a long time, he turned the phrase over in his mind, waiting for something.

Walt stepped out of the chapel. Releasing his tears had done him good, and he felt loosened. Above the blackness, in the spaces between the trees, he found the sky speckled like a trout. And, listening for it, he heard the river whispering in the valley below. They were things he could trust and the sight and sound of them buoyed him. He still had the wade upstream through the darkness toward the car. The river would be at his legs. It seemed a small burden considering what the water had given him that night.

While he stood in the darkness, another sound came to him when he stopped straining to hear the river. It was a noise that he'd been dimly aware of earlier. It wasn't like any sound he'd heard before in the woods. It droned and hummed with a measured, consistent rhythm that wasn't natural. It came from beyond the bluff above, and he guessed immediately what the source would be.

His rod caught against branches as he clawed his way up the hillside. His waders slowed him. When he crested the top, the mechanical noise was still there. He stood listening to it and feeling the sweat cooling around his ribs. In the distance, through the woods, a pale light glowed ghostly. He headed for it.

Soon, he could see it through the trees. The company had won.

They won. He stumbled out into a sudden opening in the woods. An acre of timber had been clear cut around the well site, and a dirt road disappeared toward the south into the darkness. They'd squared a twelve-foot high chain-link fence around the pump, and a street light glowed down on it from a freshly planted light pole. The ground looked wounded.

The pump made a racket resonant of the sounds that would wake him when he and his wife were young and their apartment was near a rail yard. It looked futuristic and prehistoric at the same time—the steel, birdlike head dropping down and coming up. Down and up. Down and up. Endless in its hunger. Something about its dinosaur-like build brought up ideas of extinction.

He remembered some of the arguments he'd read. One fisherman pointed out that a little used two-track would be widened into a byway for heavy trucking. Walt looked at the road again, obviously ripped in recently by earthmoving equipment. The roots of upended trees groped into the blackness along the sides of the road. He remembered something too about the risk of brine or chemical spills into Singer, Sanger, and Sauger Creeks—all three of which fed right into the South Branch. Fishermen and environmentalists argued that if the first well were successful, more would follow.

Other memories of what he'd read came into his mind. Most of Michigan's waters had once held trout—even the Detroit's Rouge River before the city began treating the stream like a urethra for all its waste and refuse. Industry had come in and made many rivers too slow, warm, and poisonous to sustain such precious life. It wasn't just the southern rivers that suffered. Fertilizer ran off from farms and golf courses into feeder streams up north. It happened everywhere in the state.

Walt thought also of the long dorsal fin on an arctic grayling, a fish he had only seen in books. It had once thrived in the Au Sable system until reckless logging destroyed its spawning habitat.

He squeezed his hands into fists. This place was supposed to be sacred, a gift. Hunching over, he searched the ground and came up with a rock the size of a softball, cold and earthy. Hurled over the fence, it clanged thunderously against the steel.

The pump kept on. Down and up. It was much stronger than

some glass-jawed Goliath. Listening for the river or for the wind, Walt heard nothing except the pump. He studied it for a long time.

He always kept a piece of paper folded in his vest pocket to write things down to remember for his next trip. During the last trip, he'd written down *tippet*, and he could feel the thin spool in his upper vest pocket. The list helped him remember. He looked at the cyclone fencing around the well site. He took out the piece of paper, unfolded it, and fished out the stub of pencil. He wrote down *bolt cutters*. Under it, he wrote *monkey wrench*.

Mercury

Branson stood in the water, alone and chilled—listening to nothing. His fly rod's four pounds felt like a length of rebar in his fist. He stared ahead, and the yellowing woods blurred around him. Blinking his eyes into focus after a time, he looked up into the patches of gray sky between the trees. The distant birds there were small shadows of restless flight. Circling. Always coming back to the same place.

A soft voice called out.

Branson turned. A man in plain clothes stood behind cyclone fencing. It was fifteen feet high with a trellis of barbed wire. Branson had fished this stretch of river before. He'd never seen the fence or thought of the closeness of the prison property to the river.

"Hi," the man said, sounding like a boy. "How's fishing?"

Branson took a calming breath. He shrugged. "Bad, like anything."

Each studied the other.

The man rubbed his chin. He smiled. "You think I could get a smoke?"

Branson touched his vest pocket. His cigarettes were there with tippet and a tube of fly dressing. He glanced at the other man.

"I was watching you." He pointed beyond Branson. "I saw you smoking upstream."

Branson nodded. He pinched the pack of cigarettes from his pocket and started out of the water toward the fence, stepping gingerly on the mossy rocks near shore. Earlier, around the upstream bend, he'd lost one of his favorite flies in some high branches. It was a pattern his son had tied. After losing it, Branson had sat on a fallen tree near the bank and picked flies from his day box and vest patch, dropping them one by one onto the river's surface until they all were gone. Nearly one hundred. He watched each one for as long as he could until the distance dissolved them. Before dropping the last one, a big hex pattern for fishing downstate rivers in June, he smirked and tied it on his line. He'd been crash landing it into some of the best holes for the last half hour.

Branson held a cigarette and the other man drew it through to his side. He had to press his face close to the links while Branson flicked up a flame. After a moment, Branson lit one for himself.

The man took a long drag and then exhaled, watching the smoke float up over the fence and melt away into the branches. "Thanks," he said.

They smoked silently. The river kept on as it had been. Branson sat and rested his stiff back against the fence. The sitting brought him some relief from what he'd been carrying.

"Catching any?"

He shook his head.

"I've seen fish feeding in there." He pointed at the river.

Branson nodded. "I've had fish out of there."

Leaves drifted down to the river and floated away.

"Used to trout fish myself quite a bit." He stared through the fence at the river. "Lived for it, really."

Branson's mind went elsewhere. The other man disappeared, as everything else had for him over the past couple days. His vision narrowed to a blurry patch in front of him and his jaw went slack. The chill came again.

"Pretty little stretch of river," the other man said.

"Hmm?"

"I said it seems like a good little river."

Branson exhaled a joyless laugh through his nose. "Seems," he repeated. "You got that right." He mashed his cigarette into the dry earth and twisted it back and forth.

The man behind the fence crouched down near him. His voice was close. "What are you saying?"

"The fish are poisoned. Can't eat them."

"How?"

Anyone who fished trout in the area knew the story. In the

1880s the Ropes Gold Mine had used mercury as its primary processing reagent. The mercury got into Deer Lake, which was the source of the river. "Deer Lake's twenty miles upstream. That's twenty miles of river. Shot."

The other man whistled. "All that from a gold mine in the 1880s?"

Branson lit another cigarette. "That and about thirty years of untreated sewage flowing into Deer Lake from Ishpeming."

"Ishpeming?"

"You never heard of it?"

"I'm not from around here."

Explaining that it was a little town over to the west, Branson threaded another cigarette through the fence along with the lighter. The other lit up and pushed the lighter back.

"Why are you fishing it?"

"It's close to home."

The man's hand was a claw where he held the fence. He steadied himself on one knee. "Do they expect that the mercury will ever get out?"

"They talk about it." Branson squeezed his right fist tightly until a knuckle cracked. He released his grip. "Everything's just goddamn talking. Lies. Nothing changes." He could feel it coming up.

The other man cleared his throat. "Yeah."

Branson took an angry drag and then exhaled. "I look in the fishing guide every year, and every year there's a black dot for this river. And every goddamn year they're talking about how it will leach out, but it doesn't. It's just pointless hoping. Not worth it." He stared at the river. He couldn't hear it through the pulse of blood ringing in his ears. "Christ," he said. He pinched his nose between his thumb and forefinger as though he meant to tear it off. His words ripped out of him like a sneeze. "He never got clean. Not really."

The other man was quiet. The river moved and smoke leaked upward from their cigarettes while intermittent yellow and orange leaves floated down off the trees around them. Everything else was still. "He?"

Branson felt it wanting out of him, like the urge to vomit after too much drinking. It would be awful, ripping, and yet he could feel it coming.

He flicked his cigarette toward the river. It didn't make it.

"Sonuvabitch." He pushed himself up, walked over to the smoldering butt, and crushed it out with his boot. He looked at the other man behind the fence. "My kid," he said. "My son."

He couldn't stop talking. Deceased wife. Son falling in with the wrong crowd and then falling away. Crystal Meth. Yes, even in a little pisshole town like this. Branson told the story of how his son had sold the switchblade—the switchblade that had belonged to Branson's father. The switchblade that Branson's father had bought shortly after being diagnosed with esophageal cancer. The old man had wanted a switchblade all his life and only bought himself one off the Internet once he received what was essentially a death sentence. Buying the knife was illegal. "What are they going to do, arrest me?" Branson's father laughed. Weakened by chemo, he clicked the blade open and retracted it for hours at a time. Having the knife seemed to give him a little strength—though not enough. When his father died, Branson got the knife, and he kept it as a reminder to himself that he should live life for the moment. Taylor, Branson's son, knew the story of the knife. He sold it anyway. He needed money. Maybe, in his deluded mind, he used the story of the knife to justify selling it.

Branson kept talking. He told about his son's weight loss—a skeleton draped in skin. He told about the arrest. And then the rehab. Depression, fear, wanting to sleep a lot, difficulty in sleeping, shaking, nausea, palpitations, sweating, hyperventilation. And then better days. And more better days. Branson had started him on fly fishing and thought that it might be some kind of new addiction that could make him forget the other. A good addiction. During the past winter there'd been the fly tying and the way his son had lost himself in it—and found himself. It seemed like every turn of thread was a stitch, making his son whole again. There was the day early in the season, in this very river, when his son had turned without a sound and collapsed into Branson in what turned out to be a long hug. It said thanks. It said I'm trying. It said this is a prayer.

Branson sniffed. "And then last week I woke up and the house was empty. A junkie friend of his said Taylor was still in town. I shook it out of the little prick in a grocery store parking lot." He held his hands out in front of him and they moved the way they had moved when he'd throttled the kid. "Told me that Taylor was using again. That he had been using for a while." He released his grip, as though he was holding more than just air.

The man behind the fence scratched his ear. He looked at the ground for a long time, pinching his lower lip. "That's tough."

Branson stood stunned from his release.

"You can't blame yourself. My old man—"

Branson held up his hand. "Look, don't feel that you have to say anything. I'm done with him. I'm spent."

The other man turned around abruptly at the sound of something moving behind him. He cleared his throat. "I should get back. I can't stay here too long. Someone will come."

"Sure." He picked up his fly rod.

The other man bent over and picked a paint brush out of the grass.

Branson looked at the brush and the yellow paint on its bristles.

"That's the job they have me on. I'm painting a storage shed. I'm on a little break." He looked behind him again and waited. He turned back and pointed his brush toward Branson. "Can I ask another favor?"

Branson smirked. "You can have the rest," he said, reaching for the pack.

"No." He shook his head. "No, it's not ... it's just that I want to know ... I want to ask you about the river."

"What about it?"

The man stepped closer. He looked over his shoulder again. "It's just that I get down here whenever I can—any time I have some kind of outside work detail. And I've memorized this one little stretch. I've just wondered ..."

Branson studied him and felt his eye twitch.

"It's just..." He took another step closer, as though he might try to walk through the fence. He pointed again, this time with the hand not holding the brush. "Up around that bend there. What does it do?"

"What?"

The man smiled. "The river. What does it do? I've always wondered. What's it like?"

Branson looked behind him at the river. He turned back and swam his hand through the air. "Just kind of snakes around in the woods."

The other's face changed, looked disappointed.

"I'm not sure what you—"

"I just mean ... is there anything else ... any other details?"

He shrugged. "I don't know the whole river."

"That's okay. Just anything."

"I can tell you what I know." He started from the trailhead where the river is fast and choppy with whitewater. The speed slows when the river splits around a long grass island, and gets slower yet when the two branches meet up again and then widen. "Lots of brookies in that riffly wider section," he said. "Good fishing." He talked of the depths in the holes and how some of them were well over his head. His son had pulled a seventeen-inch brook trout out of one. "I'm sure you know that the big ones usually stay in those deep holes during the day, but for whatever reason it came up after a little attractor pattern right on the surface. Broad daylight." Talking about trout got him talking about cover. Windfalls. Deadfalls. The overhanging banks.

"Gets strange back there, too" he said, listening to himself tell it, as though speaking it aloud were making the river real. "Last spring the winter runoff came through heavy and tore the hell out of the place. It was like three rivers coming through there."

The other man stared at the water. "There was a riot last spring," he said. "Even trustees were locked down."

Branson nodded. He explained that when the water levels had receded, the river had moved. "For about an eighth of a mile, there's just this dry river bed where the river had been. It just jumped its path."

The other man looked at the moving water. "I wonder how that happens—like it was going wrong for all those years."

Branson shrugged. He looked at the river and where it disappeared around the downstream bend. "I don't know much about the river from here down. I usually turn back here. I've heard it gets slower and deeper on its way out into the lake."

The other man held both hands in the links and looked upstream. A smile haunted his face. "You've given me a lot to think about." He let go of the fence. "I fish this stream at night."

Branson looked at him. Something in his eyes—something lost, sad. And yet something still alive. Something he had given him by simply describing a section of the river that the other man couldn't see.

Branson held his rod out after a moment. "You want me to try to catch one? You want to hold one?"

The other man smiled at the fly. "You always fish with that Pterodactyl pattern?"

Branson laughed. "I might be able to pick one up. These brookies sometimes go after anything."

The man crossed his arms and made as though to watch, smiling. Branson lit a cigarette, passed it through the fence, and then lit a second cigarette for himself. He carried his rod into the current and checked behind him for branches before casting. He used a roll cast.

The hex landed like a stone into the holes. He tried to finesse it. He smiled at his mistakes and looked at the man behind the fence. The man's face, which had been watching everything boyishly, was changed. Pale. He locked eyes with Branson and his head shook almost imperceptibly, like a leaf turning in a slight breeze. Everything about his face said no. Said don't move. Said this is really bad.

Branson stood still and soon heard the footsteps coming through the leaves behind the other man.

The man pulled his gaze from Branson and looked searchingly in the treetops.

"What the hell are you doing back here?" The new man had a rifle. His pants were black and his shirt was slate gray and crisp. He had a badge and a baseball hat with the same badge. He also had a handgun and a billy club.

The prisoner didn't stop looking up and said that he was watching the birds circling.

"For twenty-five minutes?" The guard looked up through the autumn leaves.

"It's been a while since I've seen birds circling like that. It's pretty, really," the prisoner said, pointing.

The guard didn't seem to see Branson. Branson was still, except for his heart flipping like a fish in a creel.

"You're damn lucky that Dutch didn't catch you here."

"I know."

"He doesn't buy your act, he says. He says the nice ones are the ones that eventually stab you. He's just waiting for you to screw up."

"I know."

The guard gestured with the gun. "Well, let's go."

"Okay." He didn't look at Branson again.

"So what the hell am I supposed to tell Dutch?"

The prisoner shrugged.

The guard shook his head. "Bird watching."

The prisoner went first, and the guard followed behind him.

Branson listened to their feet in the leaves. He watched them until they dissolved into the trees. He looked up. The birds were gone. It wasn't long before the sound of the river was all that was left. He stood surrounded by it for a long time, listening. Calming himself. Thinking.

He didn't stop fishing. Even with his ridiculous fly. His ridiculous chances. He took his wader belt out of one of his vest pockets and strapped it around himself. Deep water was ahead. He cast the big fly at some likely spots as he worked his way downstream. Lake Superior was somewhere at the end of the river. The mercury would never really be gone. It would settle in the lake. The lake would do its best to absorb it. Branson fished toward that body of water.